NATALIE AND THE NERD

AMY SPARLING

I'm glad Mom isn't here to see this. I press my hand to my forehead, willing away the stress headache that's slowly seeping over my skull. I begged and argued and made such a good point this morning. It was a good idea—at least I thought it was. Staying open an extra hour would mean more people could come into the store. More people equal sales.

Sales equal money.

Money means we won't lose the store.

I lower my hand and gaze around at the eight hundred square feet of gifts, trinkets, and collectibles that makes up The Magpie. It's my mom's life's work, this little gift shop. Set up right in the middle of The Vintage shopping center by the boardwalk, we are in a prime location. Right by the beach, right in the middle of all the foot traffic and shoppers who are here to visit the bigger stores and dine at the upscale restaurants.

All the conditions are perfect, yet we're about to go out of business.

I let my gaze drift to a shelf of glass angel figurines, each posed in a different way, some of them decorated with each month's birthstone, others holding a baby girl or boy, or a dog or cat. They're gifts that used to be so popular a few years ago. People would collect them for every occasion, buy one for every family member that matched their birthstone or marked an important event in someone's life. They used to be so popular we couldn't keep them in stock. I remember the November birthstone angels would sell out every other week and I'd always wonder why so many people were born in November.

One time I mentioned it and my mom snorted and said, "November is nine months after Valentine's day and that's why," a realization that made me blush from head to toe. Now I would kill to have an annoyed customer in here, tapping her foot impatiently because we're out of the angel she wants. They used to be so popular and now they just collect dust on a shelf that no one looks at anymore.

I glance at my watch. It's 7:33 and I am a total failure. The Magpie is open six days a week, from ten in the morning until six in the evening. With business dropping every month and the overwhelming stress of losing our store, which is our only source of income, I've promised my mom I would fix this place. We're no longer struggling each month. It's beyond that. We're drowning.

I came up with a genius idea earlier this morning. Today is Thursday, and just like every other week day, most people work a nine to five job, right? That means the average person is stuck at work until five and then they have to drive home, probably to make dinner for kids, or to take them to soccer practice and stuff. Our store closes at six, which means those potential customers aren't even going to bother coming in. I decided to stay open an extra hour today. Mom thought it was a dumb idea. She says our regular customers already know our hours so they won't think to come in later. I say our regular customers suck because they haven't been coming in at all lately, so why not attract new customers? Six o'clock is the time people go out to dinner at the nearby restaurants. If we're open, they'll see us and stop in.

Now I'm cringing as I recall the conversation with Mom this morning. She'd been adamant that it wouldn't work. I'd promised her it would. She left work at the usual time, a sarcastic expression plastered on her face as she walked out the door. "Have fun being bored for an hour," she'd said. It's as if she knew no one would come in, and I'd been so cocky that I'd prove her wrong.

Well, no one has come in. Score one for Mom.

I groan as I reach under the counter for my phone and purse. I'd done the best I could. I posted on the store's Facebook and Twitter pages that we'd be open later today. I even propped open the front door for half an hour, hoping people would notice it as they walked by. I can't think of a more blatant invitation to come inside than a door that's already open for you.

Heat rushes to my cheeks as I realize we probably wasted more money in electricity this past hour than we earned all day. I sling my purse over my shoulder and turn to leave just as the door opens. I freeze in place, my momentary excitement fizzling as I take in the person who just entered.

A college-age guy with cropped black hair and a tight-fitting T-shirt with the local college football team logo on it. Not to stereotype here, but he is not exactly the typical customer for a place like this. He's probably lost and looking for directions.

"Hello," I say in my polite store voice. "Can I help you?

"I hope so," he says with a laugh. He scratches his neck, glancing around the store. "My family is meeting for dinner next door and, well, I only just realized we're meeting because it's my mom's birthday."

"Uh oh," I say with a smile.

He nods, his eyes widening. "She will kill me if she knows I forgot. I texted them saying I hit some traffic when really, I was sitting in the parking lot just now, trying to figure out what to do. Then I saw your shop."

"I am happy to save the day," I say with a grin. Internally, I'm jumping up and down and shouting with excitement over this unexpected customer. "What kind of stuff does your mom like?"

"Smell-good stuff. Like air fresheners and stuff. She also likes anything sparkly."

I nod, stepping out from the counter. "We have wax melters over here," I say, pointing him toward the porcelain melters that come in different sizes and designs. "You can pick some wax cubes and put them in the tray on top. The light turns on and melts the wax, which makes the whole house smell good."

He nods, picking up one of the high-end melters, rather than the smaller cheaper ones. "She would like this. Right now she uses candles in every room, so it's kind of the same thing, right?"

"It's actually better than candles," I say. "You just turn it on and there's no fire so it's not a safety hazard. Plus, you can change out the wax scents anytime you want." I point to the shelf next to the melters where we have one hundred thirty different scents. I know this because I hand-picked each of them from our supplier, only choosing the best ones from his selection.

"This is perfect," he says as his shoulders relax. "Um...do you do gift wrapping by chance?"

"We totally do," I say. That's an extra five-dollar charge. I'm probably smiling so big I look like a freak, but I can't help myself. I'm getting a sale! A sale that will totally justify being open an hour later.

He picks out the most expensive melter ($35) and then asks me to help him choose some wax scents. I'm not exactly trying to be a sleazy salesman, but I keep showing him scent after scent, letting him see all my favorites in hopes that he buys more than one.

"I'll take these," he says, gesturing to the pile of wax cubes I've been handing him to smell.

"Which ones?" I say.

He shrugs. "All of them."

"Excellent choices," I say, scooping them up and taking them to the register. It's ten cubes in all, so another thirty dollars of profit today. Woohoo!

I wrap up the gift and make it look pretty, then I let him borrow a pen so he can sign the ($5.00) card to his mom, which I also sold him from our card section.

"Thank you so much for stopping by," I say as I hand him his receipt. This time, my cheerful smile isn't just some fake charade I put on in the name of customer service. I'm truly thrilled that he chose to spend a ton of money here.

"No, thank you," he says. "You saved my ass today."

You saved my ass too, I think. An eighty-dollar sale is a big deal to us these days. Most days, we don't even sell close to a hundred dollars total. "If your mom likes it, make sure to tell her about the store," I say. "In fact...tell everyone you know."

He laughs and gives me a little salute. "Will do. Have a good night."

"You too!" I call out as he leaves the store, the bells on the door handle jingling behind him. I can't remember the last time I had such an easy sale, and for so much money. We've always marketed to the trinket-loving crowd, and our customers are mostly middle-aged women and teachers, but maybe we should shift our marketing strategy.

Are you a crappy child to your hard-working parents? Buy them gifts at The Magpie! We even gift wrap so you don't have to do a thing but collect the praise from your overworked parents!

I chuckle to myself as I flip off the lights and lock up the store. The Vintage is a popular strip along the boardwalk in Sterling, Texas. It's been here since the fifties, and it used to be pretty famous, but then some of the stores got old and run down and people stopped coming. In the eighties, someone revitalized the strip and businesses stared moving in again. There are restaurants and gift shops and unique hobby stores for people who like model trains and comic books and stuff. A couple of the restaurants have even been featured on TV shows about quirky or unique eateries. Lately though, a few stores have had to shut down because of the crappy economy, and this rich guy named Jack Brown bought them up and turned them into businesses.

Not cool businesses like stores or restaurants, but stupid things like real estate offices or dental offices or something lame. It doesn't make any sense because people come to the boardwalk to hang out and shop, not to go see their dentist. A lot of the older store owners are annoyed by it, but my mom says there's nothing you can do. Once the little shop goes out of business, anyone can buy it and turn it into anything they want.

My mom opened The Magpie in 2001 with my dad just after I was born. Well, he's not really my dad. He's not even my stepdad anymore, since they divorced a few years ago. I was the product of a one-night stand, and my mom says she has no idea who my real dad is. She met and married Ed Reese when I was a year old, and he was the only dad I've ever known.

But now I'm glad we're not related. After the divorce, he stopped coming around. Stopped calling me. Stopped even caring that I exist. Some dad. I don't know the specifics of what made them decide to divorce, and Mom has never talked about it. Most of my friends are relieved when their parents split up because they'd been fighting for months and it was obvious they wouldn't resolve things, but that's not how it worked for me. Mom sand Dad never fought, at least not in front of me. Sure, they were kind of boring, spending their evenings watching TV on the couch, but I didn't even know anything was wrong. One day I came home from working at the store and Mom was sitting on the kitchen table.

"It's over," she said.

"What?" For a moment, I feared she was going to close the store. Sales had been doing downhill for months and it was a constant worry on my mind.

"Ed's gone."

"Oh my God," I said, fear trickling down my spine. Did the only dad I'd ever known decide to leave? Was this really happening?

Mom shrugged, her eyes never leaving the table in front of her. "It was mutual. We're getting divorced."

"Oh," I'd said, studying her face for any sign that she was heartbroken. This was a life changing thing, one of those capital B Big Deals. There was nothing sad about her though. Just my mom's normal expression; bored and a little annoyed, her short brown hair frizzy on the sides because she hadn't bothered brushing it. In the blink of an eye, my stepdad was out of my life and I never saw him again. We never talked about it. Mom just went on with life as if he'd never been there at all.

I heave a sigh as I walk home from work. My dad can disappear forever for all I care. Mom and I don't need him. I definitely shouldn't be wasting my life thinking about him and wondering what he's up to. I have bigger people to worry about.

Like Jack Brown.

2

I PULL MY JACKET TIGHTLY CLOSED. HERE IN TEXAS, IT'S USUALLY hot all the time, and it's easy to forget that sometimes we actually do get cold weather. It's the third week of February, which isn't quite considered spring yet, and it's gotten much colder since the sun went down. I did not think about this fact of weather and daylight when I offered to keep the store open another hour. In the summer, the sun stays out until at least eight. Sometimes I'll head to the beach after the store closes and then walk home, and I've never had trouble in the past. But today it's freezing, and I am an idiot. I'm wearing jeans that can hardly be called denim because the material is so thin, and a T-shirt that's even thinner than that. My sweater is more like an over shirt with long sleeves, made from a slightly thicker cotton fabric. Ugh.

My teeth chatter as I make my way up the boardwalk and down a side street toward the north side of Sterling. We live about three miles away, a fun leisurely walk in the summer time and an even quicker bike ride.

Right now I have neither bike nor leisure. I suck it up though, not wanting to call Mom to come get me. She's probably soaking in the tub by now, drinking a glass of red wine that's become as comforting to her as her late night TV shows. Of all the ways we've had to cut back on expenses in the last couple of years, the cheap bottles of wine remain on the grocery list.

Mom's not a drunk or anything. It's more of a lonely habit for her, I think. She acted fine when she split from my dad, but it's been nearly three years since then and every day she seems a little sadder. The lines on her forehead deepen ever so slightly, and her hair gets a little grayer when I'm not paying attention. Right now my mom looks like the sad woman she should have been when she got divorced. I wonder if it's all catching up to her.

Not to mention the stress of the store. I knew the struggles of a small business back when my parents were married, because they'd occasionally complain about how Wal-Mart ruins the little people and how big chains undercut them on prices. But things were good. We went on a vacation each summer and I got great birthday gifts each year. It probably helped that my stepdad had his own job on the side working for the electric company.

But now all of that is gone, and our stability hangs on each month based on how many people come into the store and choose to buy something. I think that's probably the real reason Mom is in this funk lately. It's like the more the store suffers, the less she cares. She no longer puts everything she has into keeping it running. Instead, she mopes around the place, doing a half-assed job of everything.

It's left up to me to pick up the slack. When I'm not stuck at school or working at The Magpie, I'm online, searching up ways to save a dying business. I'm learning marketing and promotion and advertising. Unfortunately, most of those things cost money. I recently had the genius idea to buy us a billboard that overlooks the beach.

Until I realized those things cost six thousand dollars.

I cringe just thinking about that day. It was two weeks ago and I was sitting on one of the benches near the boardwalk while on lunch break from the store. The billboard directly above me used to advertise the Smoothie King across the street, but now it was empty, with a big "Advertise Here" sign on it. I called the number and talked to a woman who sounded like I'd just woken her up from a nap at one in the afternoon.

"I'm inquiring about the billboard located on the boardwalk," I said, using my most professional voice.

She then dropped the price bomb on me, and she said it like it was nothing. Like people spend several thousand dollars a day on a freaking sign overlooking the city. Shell-shocked, I'd politely thanked her and said I'd call back after *speaking with marketing*. I thought pretending to have a marketing department would make me sound like less of an idiot, but it probably didn't.

That's when I met Jack Brown in the flesh.

"Hi there," he'd said, his voice booming and masculine as he sat on the other end of my bench without an invitation. "You're Marlene's daughter, right?"

Jack Brown is tall with silvery white hair that always looks like it just got a fresh haircut. He has a sharp jawline and wears tailored business suits, and although that kind of thing is totally *not* my thing, (and he's in his forties so gross), many women find him very attractive.

"Yes," I said, eying him suspiciously. I knew exactly who he was, even before he extended his hand and introduced himself. He was Jack Brown. He had billboards of his own with his face on them. I wondered how much he paid for them.

Jack Brown sold real estate for a long time when I was younger. It was one of those names you'd see on "For Sale" signs all over the city. Then he moved to billboards with his smiling mug on it, and some cars drove around town wrapped in the advertisement for his real estate company. Now, I think he just does businesses instead of selling houses. Any time a construction crew decides to tear down a piece of land and build something on it, it usually has Jack Brown's company logo.

I was not very happy to see him there on my bench.

In December, the store got a phone call with Jack Brown's company name showing up on the caller ID. I ignored the call, and then after he'd left a voicemail, I listened to it just long enough to delete it. It said something along the lines of wanting to talk about a possible buy out.

Um, not happening.

So when he met me on the boardwalk that day, I had a pretty good idea why he'd bothered to stop and introduce himself.

"How's the store?" he'd asked.

"Perfect," I said, plastering on a fake smile. "I really love working there."

"That's wonderful. I was actually hoping to have a moment to speak with your mother, but I haven't been able to get through when I call. Is there a good time to reach her?"

That's when I lied. I told him she was incredibly busy lately because we're considering opening a second store since our store is doing so well, and that Mom was often out scouting locations and too busy to work at our current store.

I don't know if he bought my pathetic lie or not, but he wished me well and then said he'd stop by soon to buy a gift for his wife.

So far I haven't seen him, which is a relief because Mom actually is at the store all day. Usually it's just her alone because I have this stupid annoyance called school that I try to attend whenever I can. The last couple of months have been kind of bad in that regard—I skipped most of December to help with the Christmas rush, and lately I seem to stay at the store once or twice a week. Like today, for example. Mom woke up with a migraine, so I offered to open the store until she felt better.

When she finally came in around eleven, it would have been lunch time at school, so I just stayed at the store. And then I didn't feel like going after all. Senior year is kind of a waste anyway. We do stuff for half of the year and then after the holidays, teachers are lazy and just ready for it to be over. I'm not missing much, and the store needs me more than school does.

I reach the Longwood neighborhood and know I'm about halfway home. It's been twenty-five minutes even though it feels like I'm walking quicker than usual. On a good day, it takes around forty-five minutes to get home. Today must not be a good day.

The only good thing is that now I'm so cold my body has kind of accepted it, and there's a numbness to my face that has stopped my shivering. As soon as I get home, I'll take the hottest shower our water heater can provide.

As much as I try not to think about Jack Brown, now he's invaded my thoughts and caused a knot of anxiety to settle in my stomach. Just after Valentine's Day, Jack called the store again. It was a Monday, but I was skipping school to work on the store's website, so I managed to get to his voicemail before my mom did.

He was much more open about his intentions this time. He offered eight thousand dollars for the store.

Anger boiled in my veins. Eight thousand dollars? That's nothing. It definitely wasn't enough money to keep us afloat until Mom found a job, which is what she'd have to do if the store closed. If he wants to offer a hundred thousand or so, then we could talk. But even then, I'm still not ready to let this store go. It's my life. It's been here since I was a baby, and I want to own it when I'm an adult. Jack Brown can piss off.

I'm still gritting my teeth by the time I see my house in the distance. Our house is two stories, narrow and long, the white paint now weathered. A shotgun style house that's just like all the others on this side of town. Our neighbors are just five feet away, and our backyard is so tiny there's no way we could ever have a dog because we'd be picking up poop for eternity.

But it's home. And it's the one thing the failing store can't take from us. Mom and my asshole ex of a stepdad bought it in cash when they got married. They'd both inherited some money from relatives and didn't want to have a mortgage. After the divorce, he let us have the house free and clear, which was nice. The Magpie earns just enough money each month to pay the rent at the store and to keep our lights on and put food on the table. One of these days, I'll make sure we're earning enough to have a great life.

Right now, I just want to warm up. It's probably a combination of being pissed about the store and being cold as an iceberg, but now my teeth hurt. I rub at my jaw as I let myself inside. Warmth envelops me, instantly making me feel better. There's a faint smell of spaghetti in the air and it makes my mouth water.

I venture into the kitchen, excited to tell Mom about my big sale, but she's not in here. There's leftover spaghetti and garlic bread on the stove, so I make a plate and then peek into the living room.

"Mom?"

She's not there either, so I call up the stairs. "Mom!"

Her door swings open, the floor creaking as she walks out and peers down the stairs at me. "There's food on the stove," she says. Her hair is messy and she's wearing a nightgown. I glance at my watch. It's almost eight, but she looks like she's been asleep. "I already got food," I say, holding up my plate. "Want to come watch TV with me?"

She shakes her head. "I'm tired, Natalie."

"Oh." My heart sinks. Since I've been spending so much time at the store this year, I've kind of abandoned all of my friends. Chatting with Mom is what I look forward to after a day of work.

"Okay, well, goodnight," I say, but she's already gone back to her room, closing the door behind her.

I sit on the bottom stair and eat my food. I'll have to get an excuse note for school tomorrow if I want to avoid getting another detention. I don't even want to go to that stupid place, but the money I made today will cover for a bad sales day tomorrow. Plus, I can work on my notebook of good ideas for the store while I'm in class. I make a mental note to write a letter saying I was sick today and then forge Mom's signature before I go to school tomorrow, and then I pack up the leftover dinner on the stove and clean up the kitchen before going to bed.

Tomorrow will be a better day, I tell myself.

It has to be.

3

My cell phone alarm is these nature sounds that start off quiet, like crickets and birds chirping, and then it slowly gets louder as the seconds pass. It's only the sounds of nature and not some stupid blaring honking sound, so you'd think it'd be a peaceful way to wake up. It's totally not.

As soon as I hear those cheery birds in the morning, I know that I have to suffer through an entire day of school and work before I reach the blissful event of sleep again.

I climb out of bed and throw on some clothes. I have only ten minutes until I meet April at the stop sign so we can walk to school. As I brush my teeth, I think back to how when school started I'd set my alarm to forty-five minutes before school so I had time to get ready and do my hair and makeup. As the months have gone by, I've pushed my alarm back further and further. If I thought I could get ready in five minutes, I totally would.

At least school is almost over. Three more months of this bull-crap and it'll be summer break, which is our most popular time of year at the store because so many people come to the beach. Since our store doesn't open until ten in the morning, I always get to sleep in late. Summer is magical.

I grab a muffin for breakfast and then rip out a sheet of paper from my notebook. In a cursive-ish scrawl that's very different from my own bubblier handwriting, I compose a letter:

> *Please excuse my daughter Natalie Reese for missing school on Thursday the 28th. She was suffering from a migraine and could not get out of bed.*
>
> *Regards,*

My pen hovers over the signature line. I've never been able to get mom's signature just right. It's like a big capital M and then some squiggles and then an R and some more squiggles. When I sign my name, I like to fully write each letter in an elegant cursive.

Hefting my backpack over my shoulder, I run upstairs and knock on Mom's bedroom door. She's awake, luckily, standing in her bathrobe in front of the TV with the remote in her hand while she flips channels. "There's never any good news on this early in the morning," she says with a frown. "I just want to see the weather, not celebrity gossip."

"Can you sign this really quick?" I shove the paper and my pen at her.

She gives my excuse note a quick glance and then scrawls her signature on it and hands it back. "They're gonna figure out you're lying one of these days," she says as I leave her room.

I don't bother replying. Unexcused absences mean I have to suffer through detention to make up missed time. If they're excused, I just get annoyed looks from the attendance lady in the office because she makes it her personal mission to hate students who miss school.

April is waiting for me at the stop sign three houses down

from mine. She's one of the only people I know who can stand around and wait for someone without killing the time on her cell phone. She says phones are stupid and nature is beautiful, but I kind of disagree. I always feel weirdly alone and awkward if I'm waiting for someone in public. The phone is my lifeline. My excuse that I'm busy doing something, to give off the look that I'm not totally awkward and alone.

"Morning," April says with a half-smile. She's only a freshman, but she seems wiser than most of the kids at school. She has long dirty blonde hair that goes all the way down to her butt and she usually lets it hang free like that. Sometimes on hot days she'll put it in a ponytail. "I missed you yesterday," she says in a way that's more of an accusation than a real sentiment. She's been pointing out my many absences lately almost as much as the attendance lady at school.

"Sorry, I got caught up at the store."

She snorts. "I don't know how you can miss so much school and get away with it."

I hold up the letter that's now folded in half in my hand. "I have an excuse."

"Mmhmm, sure." Two junior high boys in bicycles zoom past us on the sidewalk, already smelling like body odor. I feel sorry for their teachers who have to sit with them in class. April casts a sardonic glance toward my excuse note. "I'm pretty sure working at your store doesn't count as an excuse to miss school."

I shrug. "Good thing I had a migraine."

April laughs it off, but there's a serious look in her eyes that makes me feel kind of bad. It's crazy because she's a freshman, so she's basically a kid and I've almost graduated, but I look up to her sometimes. She's not only smart, but she doesn't care who knows it. She never wears makeup or fancy clothes, and she just kind of lives her life the way she wants to. I can appreciate that, even if I'm not the same way. I'm always worried about what people think of me.

We get to school just before the bell rings, which is a time-line we came up with at the start of the year. If you get here too early, you're forced to stand around and hang out. After losing most of my friends last summer because I ditched them for the store, I didn't really have anyone to hang out with. I was bitter about it for a while, but then I met April. We're casual friends – aka, friends who walk to school together and that's about it— but it turns out that's just the friend I need. Real friends get too pissy when you have to work on the store instead of go out and party with them. April doesn't party, and her school work is so important she doesn't hang out after school. It's the perfect friendship.

When the first bell rings, April nudges me on the shoulder. "Good luck," she says, eyeing the attendance lady who is already watching us as we walk down the hallway.

I laugh. "Thanks. See you after school?"

"Yep."

I step up to the attendance desk. It's like a drive through window in the hallway, and the woman's office connects into the main office. There's another guy standing there talking to her so I slip up quickly and drop my excuse note into the tray, avoiding all eye contact. I've seen so much of the attendance lady this year that I'm pretty sure she hates me on principle.

When I get to first period, I slide into my desk in the back row and ignore the idiots who are currently drawing dirty images on the dry erase board. I have no idea why high school students are such children. Would I be the same way if I wasn't so preoccupied with the store and keeping our bills paid? Maybe they're luckier than I am because they don't have to worry about those things. Or maybe I'm better off because I know how to handle real world life.

I swallow down the bitterness I feel every time I see students having more fun than me, and open up my notebook. First period is math class, and there's a warm up on the board that makes absolutely no sense to me. It must be about what they covered yesterday. I flip open to where we are studying and find that Chapter 7 looks like hieroglyphics to me. Crap. I don't understand any of this.

Mrs. Mafi begins her math lesson with a few formulas on the board that are supposed to build off of what everyone learned yesterday. Everyone but me. I take down notes and copy everything she says, but by the time class is over, I feel like I haven't learned anything. I'll have to find time to study my textbook and some YouTube videos tonight if I want any chance of doing my homework.

Second period chemistry is pretty much the same thing. Because of my horrible luck, they started a new lesson in class yesterday and I missed it. It's even more ironic, because we'd been watching science videos the two days before that, so I figured I was fine for missing class yesterday.

Wrong.

In chemistry, I sit next to two jock assholes who spend their time looking up porn on their phones and talking sports with each other. They are of no help with our lesson today. As jocks, they slide by with solid C's in every grade and it doesn't matter. No one gives me a passing grade. I have to earn them.

I sigh and sink my head into my hand as I study the elemental chart on the worksheet in front of me. We're making compounds. I can do this.

By third period, I actually do get a migraine. We're reading Shakespeare's Hamlet out loud in class and then taking a test over it. They started yesterday and are finishing up today, so I'll only get to hear the last fifteen minutes before the test. Luckily, Mrs. Hardy tells me to read the play to myself and she'll let me make up the test during lunch. I step outside the classroom, taking my textbook with me. I sit on the floor up against the wall and start reading the play. Our textbook has all these little footnotes that explain the language to us commoners who don't understand Shakespeare. I'd like to be some smart poetic person who just gets it, but I don't, so I use the footnotes a lot.

"You're Natalie, right?"

I look up and see a thin girl with braids standing over me. She holds out a pink slip from the office. "This is for you."

"Thanks," I say, taking it. I've never seen a pink slip before. The yellow ones are early release slips for when your parents come to take you to the doctor or something. I glance at it and get a bad feeling in my stomach. So now I know what the pink slips are for.

The Assistant Principal's office.

That's all it says. *Natalie Reese to AP's office.*

I chew on the inside of my lip as I make my way down to her office, the textbook still in my hand. I probably should have put it back in the classroom, maybe traded it out for my backpack, but I'm hoping that if I pretend this will be a short trip, it will be.

She probably wants to verify my emergency contacts or something.

I step into the office and show my paper to the lady behind the counter. She looks like she could be in high school herself, but she's worked here all four years I've been here, so I guess she's just blessed with younger looking skin. She tells me to wait in one of the three empty chairs outside of the AP's office.

I sit, the chewing on my lip intensifying.

Forty-five minutes pass.

The bell rings, and students shuffle into the hallways. I cringe as I think about my backpack left in the English class-room. Mrs. Hardy is a nice teacher, so she probably packed it up for me and set it to the side. My phone is in my pocket, so it's not like I have anything valuable in there to worry about.

I'm going crazy with anticipation when the door finally

opens and a creepily thin woman with short brown hair steps out. She's so thin she could be a supermodel, if you know, her face wasn't in this pinched up, severe looking pose all the time. I don't know her name, but I've seen her around the school. She wears pencil skirts and button up blouses and her hair has been cut in that same bob forever.

"Ms. Reese, come in," she says, motioning for me to enter her office. I wouldn't exactly say she's smiling, but her lips twist upwards a little.

I enter and sit down, my textbook flat across my lap. My heart is racing but I tell myself I've done nothing wrong. I don't fight or steal or cheat on tests. She has no reason to bring me in here for disciplinary reasons. Maybe it's just something stupid. Like in fifth grade when I was called into the principal's office and given a birthday card and a candy bar.

"How can I help you?" I ask, cringing when I realize I've accidentally pulled out my customer service voice that I'd use at the store. But this is not The Magpie, and she is not a customer.

The AP sits behind her desk and places her hands on top of her computer keyboard.

"The question is more of what can you do to ensure you graduate, Ms. Reese."

"I don't understand," I say, my brows pulling together.

"I would think you should understand quite clearly, Ms. Reese." This time she does smile, but it's a terrifying sight that's all sarcasm and no kindness. "You have missed entirely too many days of school this year *and* you are failing three classes. How on earth could you not understand what that means?"

I swallow as a knot forms in my stomach. Crap. I knew I'd missed a lot of school, but I didn't think was failing. "Listen…" I say, sitting a little straighter. This is one of those talks teachers have with students, trying to make them work harder so that the teacher can feel like they've accomplished something with today's youth. All I have to do is promise to do better and I'll be let off the hook and she can go on with her day, thinking she's changing the world or something stupid like that.

"I know I've missed some school, and my grades aren't that great, but I can assure you Mrs...." I look around, hoping to find a nametag on her desk. I've never been summoned to the AP before and I have no idea what her name is.

"Mrs. Reese," she supplies for me, giving me a knowing grin.

"Oh, that's weird," I say. The realization that we have the same last name makes me forget the speech I was about to give.

"It's not that weird," she says, folding her hands over her chest in a way that shows off the diamond ring on her finger. "Surely you knew it was coming?"

"Uh...what?"

She chuckles and holds out her hand to me. "Your father and I got married, silly. It's been two months, of course he told you by now."

4

———————

I stare at her so long I'm surprised she keeps the smile on her face. Of course I understand the words she's saying, because I speak English and she's talking in plain English. There's nothing to decipher here, but I don't exactly *get* it.

"Edward Reese?" I say flatly. She nods. "He's not my dad. He's nothing to me."

Her cheerful expression falls. "Well...I know it may seem different since he's not your biological—"

"No," I say, cutting her off. "He's nothing to me. He's a guy who used to be married to my mom and now he's not and apparently, he married you, but I didn't know that."

"He didn't tell you?" she says, her tight lipped smile turning into a frown.

I shake my head. "He doesn't talk to me."

She sighs, her hands folding back in her lap. "He wants to be a part of your life, you know."

"No, he doesn't." I stand up. This sudden revelation came from so far out of nowhere that I'm not sure how to process it. Who even is this lady? We've never spoken in my life and now she's married to my ex stepdad and thinks we can be friends? Um, no. "Can I go now?"

"No, dear, sit down." She motions for me to sit and I do, although I'd want nothing more than to march out of this office then out of the building and all the way back home. Although I don't care about school at all, I do care about getting into trouble, so I sit down and stay where I am.

My mind wanders back to thoughts of my ex stepdad. Has it really been three years since we last talked? He *had* reached out to me shortly after moving out. He left me a voicemail saying I can call him anytime I want. But the next day, Mom cancelled our phones and moved us to a prepaid plan to save money, so he lost our numbers. Good riddance, though. We live in the same house, so if he'd wanted to see me, he could have. Mom said it would be a huge hassle to change our last names, so we never did. I didn't really care about it because Reese is the only last name I've ever known. Now I kind of wish I had.

Mrs. *Reese*—ugh, I can't stand calling her that—begins discussing my poor attendance record. She's reading off absences from a printed piece of paper, but I don't pay much attention. I already know I've missed a lot of days. I've tried to excuse most of them because I'm sick of detention.

"So needless to say, you'll be making up time."

My head snaps up when she says these words. "I've already made up time for my unexcused absences," I say. "The rest of my absences have been excused." Detention sucks for the normal high school student, but it's even worse when you have a store to run in the evenings. I cannot waste any more of my life sitting in this stupid school.

Mrs. Reese presses her lips together. "Have you been listening, Natalie? After eighteen missed days in a semester, you're no longer covered by excuse notes. The state requires that you make up the time regardless of the reason you were absent."

My body deflates. Crap. "So how many days do I need to sit

here and waste my life when I could be working instead?" I say, the sarcasm evident in my voice.

"Tuesday and Thursday, two hours each day."

"That's not too bad," I say. Last time I had to make up time for four hours on a Saturday and that totally sucked.

"For the next two months," Mrs. Reese adds.

My jaw drops. "Are you serious?"

"I'm afraid so, dear. It's either making up time or summer school."

"And how long is summer school?" I ask, secretly hoping she'll say one week or something equally impossible.

"All summer long."

This revelation is even worse than hearing that my dad has remarried and still doesn't even talk to me. Two days a week for two months? This is total bull-crap.

I grip the textbook in my lap and struggle between totally losing my mind and screaming or trying to stay calm. I choose to stay calm. "What happens if I can't do this?" I ask politely. "Like...if I have a store I have to work at or else I'll be homeless?"

"The board of education doesn't see that as a valid reason to avoid making up time."

I frown. "Is detention still in the library?" I ask. Maybe I can spend it on the computers looking up new marketing techniques to bring people into the store.

"Yes, but that's not all. There's another thing we need to discuss."

I swear if she tells me she's about to have a baby, I'm going to lose it.

She reaches across her desk and takes a manila file out of a stack. My name is printed at the top and the edges are a little bent as if this folder is old. I stare at it, wondering if this is the infamous *permanent record* file that people talk about. I always figured these things are kept on the computer now.

Mrs. Reese sets the folder in front of her and opens it up. "I'd like to take a minute to go over your freshman questionnaire with you, Natalie."

My chest tightens as she picks up the paper inside. I totally forgot about those stupid things they made us fill out on the first day of school my freshman year. I don't even remember what I wrote on mine.

Mrs. Reese clears her throat. "The question asks what you'd like to be when you grow up. Your answer: I want to own a coffee shop in the meeting room next door to my mom's store."

I swallow. I remember that now. It's always been my dream, turning that unused section of the store into a separate business. It would have its own door on the strip but also, it'd be open to the shop so I could sell people coffee and then they could browse The Magpie.

I don't say anything, even when she takes a moment to peer at me over the top of my paper. "The next question asks how you plan to achieve your goal."

I lean forward slightly, wondering what I wrote four years ago. It was probably something stupid, knowing me.

"I will graduate high school with scholarships already won and then I will get into Sam Houston State University with my tuition either mostly or fully paid for from the scholarships. I'll complete a four-year bachelor's degree in business so that I'll be better educated to run a business and to help my mom and dad with their business."

This part hurts. Not only were my parents still married back then, but I'd had all these goals of attending college and getting scholarships. Something twists in my gut, making me nauseated. So much has changed in four years.

My mom is divorced.

I have exactly zero scholarships.

My application to SHSU hasn't even been filled out yet.

"How have your goals now changed from back then?" Mrs.

Reese asks. Her eyes watch me with a seriousness that means she might actually care what my answer is.

"They haven't changed," I admit. "I still want to run a coffee shop, but that won't happen, most likely. You need money for that kind of thing. And I'd still like to go to college, but I have no scholarships and as you've already mentioned, my grades are bad." I let out a sigh that makes my heart hurt.

"I think your goals are very achievable," she says, closing my folder and placing it on top of the stack. "I think you just got a little off track this year, but there's still a way to get everything you want."

I lift an eyebrow at her. She continues, "I'm very good friends with the admissions people at Sam Houston. They often accept students like you who had a good record with a little slip ups along the way."

I lean back into my chair. Outside, the bell rings, signaling the end of forth period. "I'm not too concerned with getting accepted as I am with paying for it. My mom and I don't have any money, and the store is more important than college anyway."

"I wouldn't say that," she interjects. "You said so yourself in your paper. If you have an education, you can run the store better. As far as finances...there are grants and scholarships, and I'm sure your father—"

"Ex stepdad," I say, throwing her a look. "And no. I will never ask him for money."

She actually looks a little sad for a minute but then she regains her composure. "I've already spoken with Sam Houston, and they're expecting your application before the school year is over. Can I tell them you'll be sending it in?"

I shrug. "I guess."

Whatever I need to say to get her to shut up.

"Wonderful." She beams. Her eyes start to sparkle a little as she leans in, as if she's about to tell me a fantastic secret or something. "I'm not supposed to go around telling students this but…" She winks at me. "I have recommended you for a scholarship and you're now a finalist for the Sterling SBA scholarship!"

"SBA?" I ask. Briefly I wonder if this woman would be so nice to me if she wasn't married to my ex stepdad. There's no way she puts this much thought into every student in the school.

"Small Business Association," she clarifies. "Since your mom owns a small business in town, the organization loves giving scholarships to students of business owners. I put your name in and they've told me you're at the top of the list. All you have to do of course, is graduate. That means pass all your classes."

I frown. "I'm not sure I will pass with how far behind I am." It sucks to admit it, but the idea of failing school is not something I want to live with. I'm not an idiot or some drop out loser. Why did I let myself screw up so badly this year? I *do* want to go to college. I want to make something of myself and earn a skill that will help me get a job if the business goes under. I don't want to live my life like Mom does, constantly stressed out about being self-employed. I hang my head in my hands. "This sucks. I didn't realize how bad my grades had gotten."

"I thought of that too," she says. She looks like she's about to tell me I won the lottery or something. "Your math and chemistry teacher are pretty set on failing you and seeing you in summer school, but I've worked out a deal with them. During your detention to make up time, you'll be in the library receiving tutoring. Tutoring for two days a week, as well as not missing any more school—" she says, giving me a long look, "will be enough for your teachers to pass you."

"Tutoring?" I say the word like it's a curse word. I can think of no worse way to spend my time after school than being retaught everything I didn't learn in class. I should spend that time coming up with ideas for the store, not listening to some old woman drone on and on about fractions.

I chew on my lip. "I don't..."

"I'll stop you right there," Mrs. Reese says, holding up a manicured hand with a wedding ring that must have cost a fortune. Way more money than it would take to keep the store afloat. "I'm afraid this isn't a negotiation, Natalie. You will attend make up time twice a week to avoid being arrested and tried by the state of Texas for truancy. You will also receive tutoring during this time period if you want to graduate and not flunk out of school in your senior year."

"I get it," I say. "Can I go now?"

"One more thing."

Mrs. Reese slides a piece of paper across her desk and then hands me a pen. "The school needs your full cooperation in this matter of truancy. Short of being hospitalized, you'll be expected to attend school every day. Do you understand?"

I nod.

"Great," she says, pushing the paper close to me. "Now sign this document saying I've warned you of the consequences of missing any more school this year."

It's some stupid thing, probably not even a legally binding contract. My eyes skim over it, the stupid wording saying I *solemnly swear* to attend every day unless a catastrophic circumstance should occur. I sign my name quickly and drop the pen on the table.

I grab my book and turn to leave. "Come see me any time you need," she calls out after me.

"Sure thing," I say, as I make a promise to myself that I'll never step foot in her office again.

5

———

I jump when my alarm goes off on Saturday morning. Is it really nine o'clock already? Ugh. Feels like I just fell asleep half an hour ago.

I sit up in bed, and the stack of papers slide off my bed with a flourish that sends them skidding all over the hardwood floor of my bedroom. Crap. I forgot I fell asleep on top of a pile of missed schoolwork my teachers gave me. Thursday had been bad enough after spending hours in the AP's office, but Friday was a freaking nightmare. Apparently, my ex stepdad's new wife had told all my teachers about my new efforts to pass senior year so I can get into college. Every teacher except my art teacher gave me a stack of missed work and worksheets they called "extra credit" that I have to finish before the year is over. The term extra credit implies that it's optional, but all of this work is not.

My teachers all spoke to me in soft tones like I was some breakable object who would shatter into pieces if I didn't get this last chance to save my grade. It's bad enough that I have to attend tutoring. Now I'm stuck doing extra work on top of that.

I don't even bother picking up the papers right now. It's

Saturday, which is luckily not a school day. I throw on a pair of skinny jeans and a pink Magpie polo shirt that actually looks kind of cute on me. It's from the time Mom and I thought about getting professional and wearing shirts with the store's logo on the front. Sometimes we wear them and sometimes we don't, but today is laundry day so I'm stuck without any other option.

Tossing my hair into a messy bun, I grab some Pop-Tarts and tell Mom goodbye. She'll be driving to the store about ten minutes before we open, but I want to get there early and get started on some ways to bring people into the store. I hop on my bike and pedal through the morning sunshine all the way to the beach.

Since I'm here half an hour early, I go ahead and flip the sign on the door to OPEN. It's unlikely that anyone will stop by this early, but just in case they do, I don't want to miss the sale. Behind the front counter, I work on the website, updating it with our new inventory and sales items. Then I type up a newsletter to send out to our pathetically small list of subscribers. We have three hundred and ten people signed up out of the eighty thousand who live in Sterling, TX. And the last time I checked, only half of them even opened our emails.

Still, I dutifully type a message to our customers, offer them ten percent off in the next seven days if they mention this email, and hit send.

Ten minutes before we open, the bells on the door jingle and I assume it's my mom, so I don't look up. But when someone clears their throat, the sound is very much masculine, and my head shoots up from behind a rack of greeting cards.

Jack Brown smiles at me. "Hello there," he says, giving me a polite nod. "I was hoping to speak with Marlene Reese."

He's dressed impeccably in a dark gray suit and shiny black leather shoes. He's holding a folder that looks somehow more threatening than ordinary folders. I glance behind him at the door, knowing my mom will be here any minute. I only have a few seconds to lie like hell and get him out of here.

"She won't be in today. I'm sorry about that." I step out from behind the greeting cards and extend my hand, figuring a handshake is a sign of professionalism. Maybe he won't call my bluff. Maybe he'll get out of here before Mom walks through that door.

"What can I help you with?" I ask.

He frowns a little, but then he hands me the folder. "I'd like to formally offer your store a buyout. I think you'll find my offer quite generous. Can you please give this to Marlene as soon as possible?"

I hold back my scowl, instead schooling my lips into a smile. "Of course. But I should warn you not to get your hopes up because my mother is still very young and has no plans of retiring or selling the store any time soon. In fact, we're considering opening up a coffee shop next door."

It's such a lie, but I pull it off pretty well. I don't even think he knows how much of a lie it is, especially since the last time I talked to him I lied about opening a second store. Still, the corner of his lips quirk up a bit in a way that reminds me of his son, Caleb. We're the same age and we even used to be friends in elementary school, though I doubt he remembers that. Now Caleb is a jock—with all the popularity that comes with it—and we're on two opposite ends of the social world at school.

Apparently, his dad and my mom are also on opposite ends. He's rich, and she's poor.

"I'll be sure to deliver this to her, Mr. Brown. Just in case she'd be interested."

"Thank you," he says, flashing me his white teeth. He really does look a lot like his son, only his son is much hotter.

"How is Caleb doing?" I ask before I can think better of it. I haven't thought of him in years, not since around fifth grade when he got too cool to sit with me on the bus. But seeing Jack

Brown this close makes me think of how much they resemble each other.

Something flashes in Mr. Brown's eyes. A recognition of some sort that makes me a little embarrassed. Maybe he remembers me from when I was a kid, and maybe he's thinking about how dorky I became and how cool his son is now. Although I'm sure business people don't think of stuff like that.

"He's doing very well," he says. "Caleb's been training for football next year. He made it into the college team for Houston. Did you hear about that?"

"Yes," I say, trying not to roll my eyes. How could I not hear it? The whole school was excited when he was drafted to play college ball. "That's very exciting for him."

"I'll tell him you said hello," Mr. Brown says as he turns to leave.

"Oh…no, that's okay," I say quickly as I walk with him to the door, resisting the urge to shove him out of it as fast as possible. "He probably doesn't even remember who I am."

"Oh, I'm sure he does," Mr. Brown says, giving me another one of his charming smiles. "I look forward to hearing from your mother."

By some miracle, my mother walks into The Magpie fifteen minutes late. I feel like spending the rest of the day dancing around and praising whatever gods have listened to my prayers. Another Jack Brown meeting has been thwarted, but how long can I keep him away from my mom? Hopefully she'll tell him to go pound sand, to shove his buyout offer up his ass. But I can't be sure of anything, especially now that the store is doing so poorly. I can't let her sell it though, so I have to keep him away from her.

"Good morning, sweetheart," Mom says. She's carrying two Starbucks mocha frappes, and I'm grateful and gleefully excited when she hands me one, but I can't stop thinking that we can't afford fancy coffee. Still, I don't say anything because she seems to be in a great mood.

"Your newsletter looked wonderful," she says, settling next to me behind the counter. We've been open fifteen minutes and no customers have come in yet.

Technically we've been open even longer than that since I got here early, but I try not to let that fact get me down.

"What's this?" Mom says, picking up the folder I'd left on the counter.

My heart leaps into my throat. "Sorry!" I say sheepishly as I yank the file from her hand. "Schoolwork. I didn't mean to leave it out like this."

Mom shrugs and checks the store's email on our computer. I breathe a sigh of relief as I shove the file into my purse under the counter. Now I can't throw it away until she's not looking.

Jack Brown's offer has increased to ten thousand dollars, which is still a huge insult if you ask me. The rest of the papers are some long contract about buying out someone's store for the purpose of selling off the inventory to the lowest bidder and turning the shop into something else. I only skimmed over it, knowing full well that we won't take ten grand for the shop where my mom has spent almost twenty years of her life.

BY SUNDAY, MY SALES EFFORTS HAVE PROVEN TO BE unsuccessful. We've only had a handful of customers this weekend, and most of them are old ladies on a fixed income who can't spend very much. A grand total of zero people have mentioned the newsletter for a discount, so I'm guessing no one actually read it.

Depression seeps into my bones by the time I start closing up shop. If good intentions could sell trinkets, we'd be millionaires.

And that's the sad thing. I don't even want to be a millionaire. I want to be a normal person with enough money to pay the bills and not stress about it. I want Mom to be happy every day, working the job she loves. I'm not asking for much here, and I don't know why I can't save the store, even with all of my hard work.

It isn't until I'm sitting in the passenger seat of Mom's car, listening to her sing along to Gwen Stefani on the radio when I realize that day it is.

Sunday.

Sunday *night*.

Tomorrow is the start of another week of school, of which I can't miss any days. Where I'm going to be thrown into classes I don't understand because I'm behind on the work. I didn't even touch my stack of makeup worksheets this weekend because I was too busy at the store.

Dread seeps into my bones, rising up until I feel suffocated by the mere thought of how much school work I'll have to do in the next two months.

I close my eyes and exhale. Deep down, I know this is a good thing because I want to go to college. I know we can't afford it and I know my grades suck and I know it might not happen, but I do want to go. I want an education in business and I'd love to open a coffee shop one day. I want to be successful enough to take care of my mom if she needs me when she gets older.

So I have to try, even if the amount of work ahead of me feels impossible.

When we get home, I get online and search for tutors in my town. I don't even know how I'm supposed to get a tutor on such short notice, since technically I'm supposed to start it on Tuesday after school. Will the school pay for it? Do I have to?

The tutoring options I find online are all pretty expensive and there's no way we can spare that kind of cash right now. Surely the school will provide someone.

Actually, who am I kidding? It's probably the teachers who do the tutoring. I'll be stuck meeting with Mrs. Hardy in the library so she can lecture me in her high pitched voice about all the things she lectures in class.

As if school wasn't already bad enough, now I'll have to do more school outside of school.

I take one look at the stack of worksheets and wish I could disappear.

6

April pulls her hair over her shoulder, inspecting the tips for split ends while we walk to school on Monday. I've been telling her about my ridiculous meeting with the assistant principal (or should I say my stepdad's new wife, ugh) and how I now have to take tutoring. It feels good telling someone about this hell I've been placed into. I can't tell my mom. She'll either be pissed or stressed out or both. Probably both.

"So now I have to be tutored by God-knows-who," I say with a groan. "If it's Mrs. Lapin I'm going to drop out of high school and become a loser for the rest of my life, I swear."

April laughs, tossing her hair back over her shoulder. "I don't think Mrs. Lapin would stay after school even if they paid her. She's always rushing out the door right after the bell rings."

"This sucks so freaking bad," I mutter. We stop at an intersection and I turn to face her, putting my hands on both of her shoulders. "Don't ever fail your classes," I tell her, looking her in the eyes. "It is *not* worth it."

She rolls her eyes. "Don't worry about me. I don't skip school unlike *some*one I know…"

There's a quick honk of a car horn, which gets both of our

attention. At the intersection, which is a four way stop sign, a red Dodge truck rolls down the passenger window.

"Is he honking at us?" April whispers as she goes very still at my side, then slides her purse around her shoulder. She keeps pepper spray in her purse, so she's probably reaching for it right now.

"Hi," some guy calls out from the driver's side of the truck. I glance around, but no one else is out here. He has to be talking to us.

"Are you talking to us?" I say because he still hasn't driven forward and this is just weird.

"Yes," he calls back, leaning over so I can see him through the window. "You're Natalie, right?"

All the air rushes out of my lungs. I don't know if I'm relieved that the car honking guy isn't some creeper asking for directions, or if I'm suddenly very nervous because I know him.

Well, I used to know him.

"Yeah, that's me," I say. Beside me, April whispers, "You know him?"

Caleb Brown motions for me to walk closer. I'm still a little surprised and confused, but my legs comply without my permission and the next thing I know I'm standing next to his truck, peering into the window.

Caleb Brown is tall like his dad, with black hair cropped short. In junior high, he kept it long and shaggy, always in his eyes. Now he's going for a more professional mature vibe, I guess. The sprinkling of freckles across his cheeks that I remember so well from when we were kids has faded into a dark tan. But his blue eyes are just as blue as I remember them.

"What's going on?" I ask.

"You own the store, right?" His brows pull together while he thinks. "The one on the boardwalk with the gifts and stuff inside?"

"The Magpie?" I offer, and he nods.

"Yeah, that one. That's yours, right? Well, your mom's?"

I nod, wondering why he cares about that. "Cool," he says, his fingers drumming on the steering wheel. "Well, um, you probably don't remember me—"

"I remember you," I say, cutting him off. "We were friends as kids."

He smiles, his lips curving into that boyish look I remember so well. "Yeah, we were. It's cool that you remember."

My insides turn to mush at that smile. I mean. Whoa. I'd had the biggest crush on Caleb Brown as a kid, but I'm not an idiot as a teenager. I know he's out of my league and way too cool and rich and popular for me to lust over now, but *wow*.

He's crazy hot.

So hot it should be illegal.

"So…you want a ride?" he says, patting the seat next to him. "Your friend can come too."

"No, thanks," April says quickly. Her soft voice makes me startle because I'd totally forgotten she was even here. She tugs on my arm. "We like walking."

I look at her like she's crazy because why wouldn't we want a ride? It's humid out here. But there's a look in her eyes that I can't ignore. She's uncomfortable with this whole thing. I can't do that to her, so I turn back to Caleb.

"We like walking, but thanks anyway." He looks a little disappointed, and I feel guilty at how much I enjoy knowing I disappointed a guy like Caleb Brown.

"It's cool," he says, recovering his features into an impassive grin. "I'll see you around."

I nod and he drives off, and I keep replaying those words in my head. *I'll see you around.* Had he said them with a little inflection at the end, like it was a question? It certainly sounded like it. Or was he just throwing out the words with no regard to their meaning, the way someone says what's up and you say fine?

I have no idea. It all happened so fast. Now I can't stop wondering what had actually happened verses what my lovesick brain wishes had happened.

"What was that?" April says beside me as we start walking again.

"I have no idea," I say, sounding breathless.

"You knew him?"

"Kind of," I say with a nod.

She stares at me in disbelief. "Isn't he like some popular jock?"

"He used to be just a normal kid, and that's when we were friends." I'm so lost in my old world of daydreaming about the past that I step on a rock and nearly trip over it. April jumps out of the way as I flail and then regain my balance.

"So are you friends now? Sorry for so many questions, but you've never talked about having popular jocks on your list of friends."

I laugh and shake my head. "We're totally not friends. That was weird." I glance around. "Do we look like we need a ride or something? Like, are we looking extra pathetic today?"

"No more pathetic than usual," April says with a shrug. "Sorry I told him no, I just didn't feel comfortable at all. You can't trust jocks. They're probably terrible drivers."

I stare at the road ahead of us as we walk. "Don't worry about it. I would have said no anyway. I mean can you imagine how awkward the ride would have been?"

She inhales a deep breath. "Exactly."

School is just as foreign to me today. The teachers all move on with their lessons while I'm still trying to catch up. I try to focus and take notes, hoping that magically the knowledge will appear in my brain as if I've known it all along.

It doesn't.

And that's the thing with education. The harder it is to learn something, the more frustrated I get, and I just want to quit. When the chemistry lesson is so freaking confusing, I don't understand a word of it, it's easier to just lay my head down and look out the window and daydream about something else. (Like how cute Caleb Brown is, for example.)

But I tell myself to try. It's senior year, I'm failing this class, and I need to get my act together.

So instead of letting my thoughts float to Caleb's sparkling blue eyes, I study the periodic table of elements. Instead of wondering why he suddenly remembered my name this morning and not last month when he'd come into the store to buy a gift for his mom, I practice listing chemical reactions.

I'm fighting a losing battle though, because by seventh period I've become totally obsessed with thinking about Caleb Brown. I've looked for him in the hallways between every class, and analyzed that quick conversation we had about eighty thousand times. What was the meaning behind asking if I wanted a ride? Did he actually remember me when he visited The Magpie that time?

Was he suddenly thrown back to his childhood when we were friends and I'd had a huge crush on him and he didn't know about it? Could he not get my face out of his mind until he remembered who I was?

I wanted to see him again, to run into him between classes and say hello and hope he'd tell me more of what was going on in his mind. Unfortunately, I didn't see him at all except during lunch. He sits at the longest table in the center of the cafeteria, surrounded by other jocks and cheerleaders and essentially every student at Sterling High who is so popular that everyone knows their names.

There was no way I was approaching him there. It didn't stop me from sneaking glances at him, though. He didn't seem to have a girlfriend, even though a girl sat next to him at lunch, stealing fries off his plate. She seemed more interested in the guy across from her, which made my heart beat a little faster. I don't even know why I care—he's not into me. There's just no way.

But I'm a stupid teenager with stupid teenage hormones that won't allow me to just live my life normally. No, I have to obsess over this gorgeous guy and the weirdly random event that happened this morning.

I'm still thinking about him when the final bell rings after school. I'm wondering if I should walk through the student parking lot instead of around it on the sidewalk. If I happen to pass by the red truck and Caleb is there, he might offer me a ride again. I'll say no out of respect for April, but still – maybe it'll give me the chance to talk to him.

I'm chewing on my lip and standing near the cypress tree where I meet April each day, still debating if I should try to find him or not when someone walks up to me.

"Hi there," the guy says. He then promptly shoves his hands into the pockets of his khaki pants.

"Hello?" I say, lifting an eyebrow. He's standing right in front of me so there's no assuming he's talking to someone else, and that's why I'm confused. Why is this guy I don't know talking to me?

Maybe he wants to recruit me into the Nerds of America club, I think, mentally rolling my eyes. He's carrying a messenger bag instead of a backpack, and wearing leather shoes with his khakis and maroon polo shirt. He's a few inches taller than me, with darker skin and shiny black hair that's gelled over to the side as if his mom fixed his hair this morning. He's like a hipster nerd—with more emphasis on the *nerd* part and less on the hipster part. In fact, I'm pretty sure hipsters would be embarrassed to hang out with him.

"Are you Natalie Reese?" he asks. He gives me what looks

like a smile, but I can tell he's a little nervous. Why any guy would be nervous around me, I don't know. Maybe he's going to try to sell me something.

But he knows my name, and that's weird. What's weirder is that now, two guys have asked me the same question today. Two guys on total opposite ends of the popularity scale.

"Yes…" I say, gripping the straps of my backpack. "I am Natalie Reese, last time I checked. Why do you ask?"

His shoulders relax a little and he gives me a smile, revealing perfectly white and very straight teeth. "Awesome. Mrs. Reese showed me your picture in the yearbook but it's really hard finding someone in a crowd based on a picture from last year."

"My mom?" I say, taken aback by the use of her being called a Mrs. when most people call her Marlene.

He looks confused. "Your mom is the assistant principal?"

"Oh my God, no," I say with more venom than necessary. "Definitely not. Ew."

"That's who I was talking about," he says, giving me a small smile. He rocks back on his heels a little. "It's coincidental that you have the same last name."

"I'd use a word more vulgar than *coincidental*," I say with a sigh. Behind him, I see April walk through the doors. I'm ready to go home and work at the store, so I need to wrap up this bizarre conversation. "So why did the AP give you my picture?" I ask.

"I wanted to introduce myself to you. I'm Jonah," he says, standing a little straighter. "I'm your tutor."

7

I GO SO STILL FOR SO LONG, I MUST LOOK LIKE I'VE malfunctioned. April waves at me from where she's standing a few feet away. Concern is stitched all over her face, and she's got this questioning look like she's wondering if she should walk home without me, or maybe tell a teacher that I need help. I shake my head at her and hold up a finger, signaling for her to wait.

"You're my tutor?" I ask, giving the guy a look over. "But… you go to this school?"

He stares at me like I might not be quite right in the head and then nods. "I'm Jonah Garza…I think we had a class together in junior high. Your name seems familiar."

I swallow as I take in his features. Neatly trimmed hair, clean fingernails gripping the strap of his messenger bag. There's the faint scent of soap coming from him, and now it all makes sense. Jonah Garza.

He was the biggest nerd of elementary school. Always dressed in neatly ironed clothes, his hair always combed to the side and gelled in place. He was a world class dweeb, and such an easy target for bullying that the meanest bullies just left him alone. It wasn't worth it to pick on someone so obviously dorky. I mean, where's the skill in that?

We were never really friends, Jonah and I. But we have had some classes together. He must have learned how to blend into high school because I can't remember ever seeing him around campus.

"You can't tutor me," I say, meeting his concerned look with an annoyed one of my own. "You're a freaking student."

"You're a student too," he says, the corners of his lips twisting into a grin. "I've been tutoring my peers since freshman year. Mrs. Reese gave me a rundown of your situation, so I'm all ready to begin tutoring tomorrow. Just wanted to introduce myself today so you'll know where to find me in the library after school."

"Wait—No." I hold up my hand and shake my head. "I'm sorry but, um, yeah no."

"You okay?" Jonah asks.

I can't even find the words to describe exactly now *not* okay I am right now, so I brush past him and march back toward the school.

"Nat?" April calls out.

I give her an apologetic look. "Can you wait like five minutes for me? I have to go settle something in the office."

"No problem," she says, leaning up against the brick wall.

I head into the school, walking as fast as I can through the wave of students all trying to get out of the building. I hear Jonah call my name from somewhere behind me, but I don't stop to answer him.

I walk as fast as my feet will take me until I get to the double glass doors of the office. Two teachers are eating cupcakes in the lobby and I step around them.

"Natalie!" Jonah calls. I glance back and see him slip into the office, his eyes wide.

"You can come if you want," I tell him. "I don't really care either way."

The assistant principal is sitting behind her desk in her office, her eyebrows pulled together while she stares at something on the screen.

I don't bother knocking, I just walk right on in, throwing my hands in the air. "I can't be tutored by a student!"

She startles at my sudden appearance, nearly knocking over a half-empty coffee cup on her desk. "Crap!" she breathes. She puts a hand to her chest. "Natalie, you scared me. What on earth is going on?"

Her eyes flit from me to Jonah, but she still doesn't get it. I repeat myself. "Jonah can't be my tutor. He's a student."

"I'm not sure I understand," she says, folding her hands together over her chest. "Do you and Jonah have a personal conflict that would prevent you from working well together?"

"No ma'am," Jonah says. "We don't even know each other. I'm happy to work with her."

I shoot him a look and he flinches. "Mrs...." I exhale and realize I'm going to have to call her by her name. "Mrs. Reese, you said I'd have to be tutored but you didn't say it would be by a student. I thought you meant someone professional."

Her lips form a flat line. "Honey, peer-to-peer tutoring is how it's done in high school. You're free to hire an outside tutor all you want, but for school purposes, we always match students up with other students. In fact, most of them prefer it this way. Isn't tutoring with a friend better than with a teacher?"

"He's not my friend," I say without thinking. I turn to Jonah. "No offense... I just don't know you."

He shrugs.

I look back at Mrs. Reese. "I'm just not sure I want to be tutored by a fellow student. We're the same age...it's just...insulting."

She barks out a laugh and then quickly composes herself. I

grit my teeth because while I don't appreciate being laughed at, I know I should probably keep my cool right now.

"Natalie, you may be peers in age but Jonah is well equipped to tutor you." She turns her gaze on him. "What's your GPA, Jonah?"

"Four-point-zero, ma'am."

"And yours is hovering around the two-point-zero range if I recall," she says to me.

My cheeks flush red, which is another example of why I shouldn't be tutored by a student. It's embarrassing that he knows how badly I'm failing my classes. If I were taught by a random adult, I wouldn't really care.

I heave a sigh. "I guess I'm not getting out of this, am I?"

"Of course you can get out of it," she says rather sarcastically. She picks up her office phone and puts it to her ear. "Let me just call the local McDonald's and see if they're hiring a high school dropout. Maybe in twenty years of hard work, you'll be able to make assistant manager."

I scowl as my cheeks turn even redder. "I get it," I say with a sigh.

She smiles but it doesn't reach her eyes. "Jonah, you let me know if she gives you any trouble."

"Yes, ma'am," he says. I shoot him another look and he pales. I can tell he wants to apologize to me for being rude, but he won't because he's in front of an administrator.

I hold back an eye roll of epic proportions and walk out of the office, not caring at all if Jonah is following me this time.

I'm steaming mad and horribly embarrassed, and as if having detention twice a week for two months wasn't bad enough, now I have to spend it being tutored by a nerdy guy who's the same age as me.

What kind of crap is that?

It's not like I'm some druggie delinquent who skips school to get high and break into cars. I'm trying to take care of my mom here. But the school doesn't see it that way. They don't care if my intentions are noble, they only care that I can memorize chemistry equations that I'll most certainly never need in real life.

The hallways are nearly empty now and I walk a little slower on my way back toward the parking lot. All of my energy has been zapped from that conversation with the woman who married my ex stepdad. This whole situation just blows.

I hear his footsteps jogging to catch up with me but I don't acknowledge him, not even when Jonah falls into step next to me. He does smell pretty good for a nerd. Most guys smell like sweat from athletics or like too much of that cheap men's body spray. But not Jonah. He smells like clean. Like he just showered. He looks so put together, so organized and creased. He probably never smells dirty.

"I'm sorry about this," he says beside me. "I tutor to make my college applications look good, and they just call me in and tell me who to tutor each week. If it makes you feel any better, I think I'm the best one out of the other five student tutors."

I look over at him and he's smiling, his dark eyes crinkling at the corners. "Why do you say that?"

"Well, one of them is Justin Mark."

I curl my lip. Justin Mark was a very large guy until two years ago when he got weight loss surgery. Now he spends every waking second talking about his workout regimen and how much weight he's lost from day to day. Even the teachers always tell him to shut up.

"You're definitely better than him," I say.

Jonah's smile widens. "The other tutors are girls. The Khan twins, Tamera Blight, and Jess McGovern."

I stick out my tongue in disgust. "Wow. Yeah. I dodged a bullet here."

Those girls are always fighting to be the smartest in the school, and oddly they're all very popular. The Khan twins are also cheerleaders, which kind of defies the whole dumb cheer-leader stereotype. They're all into makeup and fashion and school work. I wouldn't fit in with them at all.

I guess Jonah Garza is the best tutor I could have ended up with, all things considering. I turn to him, trying to force myself to think positively. "Will you be my tutor the whole two months, or will you switch off with the others?" We reach the doors at the end of the hallway and he pushes it open, waiting for me to go first.

"It's up to you. If you don't like working with me after a while, you can request another tutor."

"No, thanks," I say. "I think I'll keep you."

It could be my imagination, or some kind of trick of the sunlight as we step outside, but it almost looks like Jonah's cheeks turn a little pink. April steps away from the wall and joins us. She's still not on her phone, which is so weird to me.

"You ready?" she asks me.

"Yep." I turn to Jonah. "So I guess I'll see you tomorrow?"

He nods and adjusts the strap of his messenger bag. "Three p.m. sharp or I'll make you write five hundred sentences about the importance of being punctual."

"Seriously?" I balk.

"No." He grins sheepishly. "I'm just messing with you."

8

I TRY TO PAY ATTENTION IN CLASS THE NEXT DAY.

I swear I try.

Each class is like one new nightmare after another, with lessons that don't make any sense and teachers who talk too fast, but none of that is what's bothering me. I can't stop thinking about what happened last night while eating dinner with my mom.

"I wonder if I should just get a job," she had said, pressing her fork to stand up in her bowl of spaghetti.

I nearly choked on my own dinner. "You have a job, Mom."

She sighed. "I'm talking about a real job. Maybe I should fix up my resume and start sending it out places."

My heart sped up in my chest. "You mean like over summer break?"

She shrugged and twirled her fork around the noodles. "Or now."

"But then who would run the store while I'm at school?" I said. I refused to believe that she meant what it sounded like she was saying.

"We'd just close the store." She said it simply and easily, as if it wouldn't be a big deal at all.

I looked down at my food. "You don't mean that."

She sighed and went back to eating. I didn't say a word and neither did she until her bowl was empty and she stood up to take it to the kitchen sink.

"I guess you're right," she said softly as she walked by and headed toward her room. "I'd be lost without the store."

Now, as I sit in my chair at the back of the history classroom, I wonder how often my mom has thought about closing the store and getting a job. The very idea of it sends a weird mixture of emotions through me. I'd be heartbroken to lose The Magpie. There's no way around that.

But if Mom really wanted to close it? If it would make her happy to get a normal job working for someone else without the stress of running her own business? I guess I'd be okay with the idea, so long as it made my mom happy. But I know that deep down she wouldn't be happy at all. And she's only thinking these things because money is tighter than tight and the store is doing worse than it ever has. I close my eyes and draw in a deep breath, pretending I'm on a tropical beach instead of in the classroom listening to a lecture on Texas History.

It doesn't work very well.

As much as I want to forget all about my first tutoring session today, I know the AP would have my ass if I skipped it. I even remembered to bring along the stack of extra credit worksheets my teachers gave me. I've put them in a folder and all together, it's about an inch thick. There is no possible way I'll ever get through them all.

Lugging my textbooks along, I make my way to the library after the final bell rings.

Sterling High's library isn't as modern and large as some of the other high schools I've seen on TV, but it's okay. The aisles are long and tall and filled with books that actually have interesting material in them, unlike the library at our junior high which is from the seventies and has mostly old smelly books.

I chew on my lip as I look for Jonah in the crowd. Most people are here for detention, which takes place in a classroom off the side of the library. To the right, the rows of bookshelves split in half and there's a few tables in the middle of the library.

I find Jonah sitting at one, bent over his iPad. He's got a TI-84 calculator next to a fresh notebook and pencil sitting next to him. His messenger bag is on the seat to his left, so I go to his right and dump my backpack on the floor.

"Hey." I pull out the chair and sit next to him. "What are you so enthralled with?" I ask, leaning over to peek at his iPad. I was hoping for some juicy snapchats or something, but no, of course not. He's looking up microphones on some website.

"Hi, Natalie." Jonah smiles at me, his eyes meeting mine. It's such a friendly gesture it makes me feel bad for how much I totally hate that I have to be here with him for two hours. It's not his fault he got stuck as my tutor. He probably doesn't want to be here any more than I do.

Jonah closes the leather case over his iPad and tucks it into his messenger bag. "You ready to get started?"

"Not really," I say, grabbing his calculator. "Let's do something else."

"Something else?" he says slowly. I press random buttons on the calculator, and he watches me, looking as though he'd really like to tell me to stop. He's such a nerd he can't even ask for his calculator back. I roll my eyes and set it on the table.

"Yeah, something else." I look around conspiratorially. "How about we sneak out of here and go get a snow cone next door?"

He frowns. "Natalie, we have to study."

I give him my best innocent look. "Or we could not study and pretend that we did?"

He ignores me and turns to his notebook. "You're failing math, chemistry, and history," he says, pointing at each subject as he says them. "You're also hovering by with a seventy-one in English so we should work on that one, too."

"What is this?" I say, snatching the notebook from his hand.

"Hey!" he says, but his voice is meek because we have to be quiet in the library. I know he's too nice to steal it back from me, because all nerds are too nice. I almost feel a little bad at how his manners restrain him so much.

I stand up so he can't even try to grab the notebook back. He doesn't leave his chair, but he is staring at me, his dark eyes more serious than I've ever seen them.

I look over the page in front of me. My name is at the top, handwritten in neat letters.

He's listed out my classes with my last progress report grade next to them. No doubt this information was given to him by the assistant principal, much to my chagrin. He's highlighted my failing subjects in blue and English in yellow. That must be his code colors for MISERABLY FAILING and ALMOST FAILING.

Underneath that, he's written the dates we're tutoring.

"Natalie, please," Jonah says, his voice one level above pleading. "Please give it back."

I shake my head and turn to the next page, finding another student's name and grades, as well as their tutoring schedule.

The pages before mine are filled with more of the same, only these must be old students because after the original grades, he's written in new grades which are much higher than what they started out with.

"Natalie…" Jonah says. "Sit back down. Let's get started."

I'm starting to feel a little bad for stealing his notebook and goofing around when we should be working, but I can't help myself. No one actually takes these things seriously, right?

I walk back to my chair and flip the notebook to my page. That's when I notice the upper right hand of the page has been dog-eared.

Jonah reaches for the notebook. "Hand it over, please."

I flip up the corner of the page. In tiny handwriting, he's written another note, but this one is slanted and rushed, like a quick note to himself.

brown hair
Short
Pretty

I look up and find Jonah staring at his hands. His cheeks are pink and he's clearly mortified that I saw his note to himself. I hand the notebook back to him and then sit in my chair.

"Thank you," he says quietly as he reaches for a math textbook. "We can start with math, since that's often the hardest subject. After this, the other subjects will feel easy."

"I'm sorry, I can't let this go," I say, leaning back in the padded library chair. He looks at me, lifting an eyebrow. "You think I'm pretty?"

His ears turn redder than a stop sign and he looks down at the textbook in front of him. "We should focus on schoolwork."

"Come on, Jonah," I say, nudging him in the shoulder. "That note was about me, right? You probably wrote it after Mrs. Reese showed you my picture as a way to remember what I looked like?"

His jaw works but he doesn't say anything. He also doesn't look at me, choosing rather to stare at page 312 in the book. "Can we please get started on the work?" he asks, still not looking at me.

"Fiiiine," I say with a sigh. "I'll drop it. It's just that no one's ever called me pretty before so—"

His head snaps up, his eyes shining with disbelief. "That's not true."

"Uh, yeah it is," I say sarcastically even though this topic makes my chest hurt. "I think I would know."

Some of his initial embarrassment has faded away, now replaced with pure skepticism. "There's no way you've gone your whole life without being called pretty."

I nod quickly. "I'm serious. I mean, okay, maybe my mom has said it once or twice, but she doesn't count. As far as guys go, it's never happened."

I cast a glance at his notebook. "Unless you know, you want to admit you wrote that note about me."

His bottom lip pulls under his teeth. "I bet every guy in this school thinks you're pretty. If you haven't heard anyone say it, you're just not listening. Probably the same way you don't listen to teachers in class."

Something in the way he makes this bold statement, all matter-of-factly and with no hesitation at all, makes my stomach flutter. I meant it when I said I've never heard those words from a guy before. Once, last year, I was wearing leggings with a shirt that wasn't long enough to cover my ass and Jeremy Rodriguez yelled out, "Dang, Natalie! That backside is fine!" But in no way shape or form is that considered being called pretty.

"Well, believe me or not," I say with a shrug. "No guy has ever told me that, so your note has totally made my day, whether you wanted me to see it or not."

He clears his throat and focuses back on the task at hand. "So…math first?"

I shrug. "It's up to you. You're the smart one out of this duo."

"Math it is. In two weeks, you'll be having a cumulative test over the third quarter lessons in the book, so I printed out a few practice exams. I figure we can go over them together and whichever ones you have trouble with will tell us what to focus on studying."

He talks quickly, his lesson plan already mapped out before we sat down today. After going over his plans for math with me, he moves to chemistry and history, where he's put together study plans just like this one.

I watch him silently as he tells me all about the lessons and practice exams and gives me insight on how my teachers grade the midterms which are coming up soon. It blows my mind how smart he is, and we haven't even officially started studying yet.

He's still talking, reciting several pre-cal equations out loud as he writes them down on a sheet of paper. I try to focus, but I can't help myself.

"Does it hurt your brain being this smart?" I say between watching him write one equation to the next.

His dark eyebrows pull together. "I don't know how to answer that."

"You're incredibly smart, Jonah. My brain hurts just listening to you talk. Surely your brain hurts, too, doing all that thinking?"

He shakes his head, looking at the paper in front of him. I've noticed that a lot about the last half an hour we've been working together. If he can look at his paper instead of me, he does. I wonder if he thinks I'm *pretty*, pretty, or just normal pretty. Just like he wrote the word pretty to mean I wasn't some hideous monster roaming the hallways.

"My brain feels fine, Natalie." He covers up the top part of the paper. "Can you recite to me the quadratic formula? Mrs. Mafi gives five extra points if you write it on the top of your test."

I sigh and rest my chin in my hand. "This is going to be a long two months if all you want to do is talk about school work," I say.

"What else would you suggest we talk about?" This is the

first hint of friendliness he's had since we started the tutoring session.

"Tell me your favorite color."

He grins, then looks back at the paper. "Get an A on your next test and I'll tell you anything you want to know."

9

THUNDER CRACKS OUTSIDE, SENDING A *BOOM* DOWN THE ART hallway on Thursday. Yesterday was overcast and humid, which made it horrible walking home from school. Today, our crazy Texas weather decided to really give us the finger. It's been thunder storming outside since first period began.

Luckily, April and I made it to school before it started raining. Nothing sucks more than being stuck sitting in class with soaked clothes. It's happened twice since I started high school, which isn't bad considering how many times I've walked to school. The junior high is only a block away from my house, so walking there was a lot easier. If it was raining, I'd just wait five minutes until it stopped and then run to school.

April turns the corner from the main hallway. She also has art for sixth period, but she's in ceramics class and I'm in painting. She's got her nose stuck in a paperback book, so she doesn't realize when she's about to knock right into me.

"Uh, excuse you," I say rudely—but in a playful rude voice. She must not realize who I am because she startles and looks up, her eyes big like she might pass out from fear of colliding with a senior. Then she recognizes me and her shoulders relax.

"Sorry," she says, shoving her bookmark back in her book. "This rain better let up before school is over."

I groan. "If it's not, we're just gonna sit inside until it stops. I can't stand the idea of getting soaked on our walk home."

"Hey there."

April and I turn to see who just joined our little group in the hallway. I nearly crap myself when I see Caleb Brown approaching, that one-dimpled grin on his face. It's been two days since he stopped us on the road before school, and I haven't seen him since.

"See you later," April says, slipping past me. She is so weirded out by guys, the poor thing. I can't even tell her bye because she leaves so quickly.

I swallow my nerves, but it doesn't help at all. "Hi, Caleb."

He's wearing dark skinny jeans and a black shirt underneath his letterman jacket. It's not even that cold outside today, but he looks good, so who am I to complain?

"It's really pouring out there," he says, giving a quick glance over his shoulder to the set of glass doors at the end of the hallway. The sky has turned an angry gray, and the rain is so thick you can barely see the football field outside.

"Yeah, it sucks because rain always makes me want to fall asleep in class."

He chuckles, then leans forward, his head lowering just inches away from mine. "So take a nap."

I stiffen. He smells a little like cologne, but also like something leathery, like he's just left a car wash. "I wish," I say, trying to sound sarcastic, but the truth is so real it makes my stomach hurt. "I can't goof off in class anymore. My grades suck."

"Nah, I don't believe that," he says, standing back to his full height. "You look smart."

I resist the urge to tell him how terribly wrong he is. I have no idea why Caleb Brown is talking to me in the hallway, but I'd like to keep it going as long as possible. "So what class do you have next?" I ask.

"Athletics," he says. "So, Natalie..."

The way he says my name sounds like he's been thinking it over for a while. Now that he's clearly about to ask me something, all the sounds in the hallway fade away until it's just me and Caleb standing here face to face. I know it's too early to expect him to ask me on a date but...what if he does?

"Yes?" I say, my voice barely a whisper.

"Since it's monsoon season outside, I figured I could give you a ride home today."

Oh. My shoulders fall. So that's all he's asking. Of course, it's better than nothing. But I can't leave April to walk home in the rain and she most likely won't want to ride with him either. I'm about to tell him that when Jonah Garza interrupts the conversation.

"Hey, Natalie," he says, flashing me a nervous smile. He's holding a ceramic vase in one hand and a stack of papers in the other. I'd been so caught up in staring at Caleb's gorgeous cheekbones, that I hadn't even noticed Jonah walk by. "We still on for today?"

All of the excitement I'd had just seconds ago bursts into flames in my mind. Dammit. I have tutoring today. How could I have forgotten that?

"We're still on," I say, trying not to heave the world's largest sigh.

"Cool." He smiles, his eyes crinkling in the corners. He doesn't even seem to notice Caleb standing there. "See you at three."

After he leaves, I turn my attention back to Caleb. He looks annoyed...or maybe...jealous? There's no way.

"So, you got plans with nerd boy?" Caleb asks, the irritation obvious in his voice.

Oh snap, is he jealous? *Is he seriously jealous?*

I am freaking out on the inside, absolutely losing my mind. Caleb Brown just asked to drive me home, which is basically a precursor to asking me on a real date. And then Jonah ruined it and Caleb actually seems jealous.

"Yeah, sorry," I say, deciding to maintain an air of mystery instead of letting him know I just have tutoring. "I'm busy after school. But thanks so much for offering me a ride." I grin and touch his shoulder with as much confidence as I can muster, even though my knees are shaking. "You're such a sweetheart."

With that, I turn and walk straight into my classroom, feeling as though my heart will explode. I cannot believe I just boldly flirted with Caleb Brown. My grades may suck, but right now my social life is totally on point.

"So," Jonah says when I join him at the same table in the library after school. "Show me your stack."

I put a hand to my chest. "Ugh, Jonah. That's a little forward, don't you think? Maybe buy me dinner first?"

He looks confused for just a second and then he blushes and presses his lips together. God, I love how easily I can make this nerd blush. He's probably never even dated a girl, much less flirted with one.

"I meant stack of *papers*," he says. "Not...well—I don't even know what the word stack could mean in another connotation."

I shrug. "It sounds kind of like rack?"

He gives me this incredulous look. "You don't even know the meaning of your own joke?"

"What can I say?" I reach into my backpack and dig around inside. "If I can find a way to crack in inappropriate joke just to see you blush, I will."

"You are ridiculous," he says with a long exhale. "I'm not

blushing. If anything, I'm red with rage because you're the most annoying person I've ever tutored."

"Dang, Jonah!" I put a hand to my chest. "Bringing out the claws, huh?"

"Sorry," he says quickly. "Show me your *papers*. How much did you get done?"

After our session on Tuesday, Jonah had looked over my stack of extra credit worksheets and said I should be able to do at least ten of them by the time we met again. Ha. Yeah. Freaking. Right.

I managed to do three of the easier worksheets after dinner last night, and that's all I've done.

I hand him the stack of papers, hoping he won't actually go through them.

But of course he does.

"Three?" he looks up at me and I expect a lecture or some other look of disappointment. Instead, his brows pull together in concern, "Is everything okay?"

His question hits home, but I'm not about to tell this guy anything about my stressful life away from school. I shrug like I don't give a crap. "Yep."

"Okay," he says, turning his attention back to the papers. "You need to finish five a day to complete them all in a month. At this rate, you'll be done in two months or longer."

"Well, they didn't give me a due date," I say.

"Don't underestimate how long it takes the teachers to grade these. I'd get them in as soon as possible. If they aren't graded by the end of the school year, you'll be SOL."

"Oh, awesome," I say sarcastically. "Now I'm even more stressed out about this crap." I take the papers from him and shove them back in my bag. "Can we just get to the tutoring now? I promise I'll work on the stack when I get home."

"Don't get tripped up if the questions are confusing," he says, still talking about the stack of extra credit work. "Just circle it and skip over it and we'll look at them next time we meet up, okay?"

"Sure thing, Boss."

I feel a little bad for how sarcastic I am during the duration of our tutoring session. But I really can't help it. Jonah is so hyper focused on work, work, work, and he never wants to joke around or get off topic. He's just so serious all the time. And the worst part? That look in his eyes when he bothers to take his focus off the papers in front of him. When he truly looks at me, I see something reflecting back on his features that scares me a little.

The boy genuinely wants me to succeed. It's not because we're friends or anything, because we aren't. It's probably just because every person he turns from a failure to an honor roll student looks good on his college applications. But I can see it plainly on his features: he wants me to succeed.

And that's just too much pressure for me.

What if I still fail? What if I screw up, not only my chance of graduating without summer school, but his record as well? I'd hate to be the only student in his notebook whose grades didn't improve after working with him.

"So, I thought we'd work on chemistry today," Jonah says, pulling me from my thoughts. As always, he's been talking this whole time and I haven't been listening.

"I hate chemistry," I say with a groan.

"I know, but you have a test on Monday. It'll be here before you know it."

"Seriously?" I say, and then I cringe because I totally said that way too loud for the library. I look over at the librarian and she's staring at me. Oops.

"Natalie, what are you doing in class besides listening to the teacher?"

I pick at my cuticles. Today in chemistry, they were going over some five-page worksheet—which I now realize was probably the test review—and it was all so stressful I spent most of the time on my phone, trying to spruce up The Magpie's Facebook page. When I tell Jonah this, his jaw falls open.

"I know, I know," I say, holding up a hand. "I am the worst student ever, and if I want help and must also help myself, and your tutoring record will be ruined because of me, and you hate me."

"I don't hate you," he says quickly. "I'm not thinking any of that. I'm trying to think of a good way to teach a student who doesn't want to be taught."

He looks off into the distance and then his face lights up. "I've got it. Come with me."

I follow him to the back of the library to a row of computers that face the back wall. "You really hate studying the textbook, so I think a computer lesson might really help you. Plus, you can do it at home."

He pulls out a computer chair and motions for me to sit. He leans over me and turns on the computer screen, then opens the browser. "Have you heard of ChemXLabs?" he asks.

"You smell good," I say.

I clamp my hand over my mouth. I did *not* mean to say that. *Oh my God, Natalie, what are you thinking?*

I mean, I know exactly what I was thinking. I was thinking that Jonah is hovering over my shoulder and he smells like soap again and it's such a nice smell compared to guys like Caleb who have got it going on in every possible way, yet they smell weird.

Jonah ignores my comment, which is probably for the best. He pulls up the school's website and then clicks on the links for students. ChemXLabs is on the list.

"I've heard of it, but I haven't used it," I tell him.

He clicks on the log in then releases the computer mouse for me. "Just log in and I'll show you how to set it up. You can pick the chapter you're studying in chemistry right now and it'll give you practice tests that pretty accurately match the one you'll get in real life."

"How do I log in?" I ask, looking back at him.

"It's just your school log in for all of these websites."

My lips squish to the side of my mouth. His eyes widen and he puts his hands on his hips. "You've never logged into these sites before?"

I shake my head.

"In all your four years of high school?"

I lift my shoulders and bite my lip, trying to look somewhat innocent. He rolls his eyes. "It's SHD in all caps, and then your birthdate. The password is SHD2017. That's the same username and password you can use to sign into all of these *very* helpful school approved study sites," he says. "You might want to write it down and use it sometime."

"Thank you, Mr. Garza," I say sarcastically. "You're so smart and helpful."

He doesn't respond to my sarcasm, of course I didn't expect him to.

"So my username is SHD," I say, typing in the letters.

"And then your birthday in month, date, year format," he says.

"April third..." I say, looking at the keyboard.

I type in my username: SHD04032000 and then the password, and what do you know, it works. Jonah finally takes a seat in the rolling computer chair next to me and he walks me through how to set up the chemistry lesson that we're studying in class. The website is pretty good, as far as something boring like studying goes. We spend the rest of our time working the questions online and taking a few of the practice tests.

By the time we're finished, I actually feel like I might know some stuff about chemistry now. No, I feel better than that. I feel like I'm going to pass the test.

"Thank you for showing me that website," I say as we gather

our things and log off the computer. "I'm feeling pretty confident for the test on Monday."

Jonah grins, sliding his messenger bag over his shoulder. "Let me know how it goes, okay?"

"You'll be the first person I tell," I say. Then I give him a wink just to see if he blushes.

He totally does.

10

In a strange turn of events, my mom goes to the store early on Saturday morning. She'd asked if I wanted to ride with her, but I was tired and needed a shower so I said no. By the time I arrive on my bike, it's twenty minutes before the store opens and my mom is in a wonderful mood. I find her humming to herself while she erases the outdated message on the chalkboard easel we keep outside the store.

It's such a drastic change from her usual gloom and doom mood that I'm not sure how to handle it. I park my bike at the nearby bike rack and lock it up with my neon green bike lock that I've had since sixth grade.

"Good morning, Mom," I say, trying not to act too surprised by her good mood out of fear of sending her back into a bad one.

"Hi, sweetheart!" Mom's short brown hair is pulled into a tiny ponytail at the back of her head. The little strands of hair up front are pulled out of the way with a black headband. She looks younger with her hair like that. Or maybe it's the smile on her face that takes a decade off her appearance.

"I've got great news," Mom says, her eyes flashing excitedly as she turns back to the chalk board. She takes a chalk pen and shakes it back and forth before uncapping it. These pens are really cool because they're liquid chalk, which lasts a lot longer than normal chalk. Plus they're more fun to write with.

"What's the good news?" I ask.

"It's not good news, it's *great* news," she says. She leans back to let me see what she's writing on the board.

NOW AVAILABLE, she's written in big block letters.

Anticipation ratchets up in my chest as I watch her write each letter of what's "now available" at our store. When she's finished, she turns to look at me, her expression so hopeful it makes me feel really bad for what I'm about to say.

"Bestselling books?" I read the sign again to make sure I hadn't imagined it. "What does that mean?"

"Natalie," Mom says sharply as she stands back up, capping the chalk pen. "I don't need sarcasm or cursing. Come inside and help me unload the boxes."

And boy, is the front of the store filled with boxes. There is also one new and rather large dark wooden bookshelf right as you walk into the store. It's about ten feet long and taller than I am. I gaze around at the scene, so weirdly confused it makes my head hurt. "So we're selling books now." It's a statement and a question and confusion all wrapped up in one.

"Yep!" Mom claps her hands together, then she takes a pair of scissors to the first box on the stack. "Only the bestselling books, of course. I've ordered five copies of the top twenty New York Times Bestselling books."

I try really hard not to slam my head against the wall in frustration as Mom starts opening the boxes. "You know bookstores are a dying business, right?"

Mom rolls her eyes. "That's why we're selling only bestseller books. They've already proven that people like them, so we'll be offering books people actually want. Plus, we're not a bookstore. We're a gift store that also has books."

"But people buy books they want from actual bookstores," I say, taking the handful of new hardbacks she gives me. "Or, more accurately, they buy them on Amazon."

Which is why bookstores are going of business, I want to say. But Mom has that look on her face that tells me she won't listen to anything I have to say right now. She's the parent and she knows best. At least, that's what she thinks.

"Natalie, this is a good idea," she says as we work on filling up the new bookshelf with the new merchandise. "We're a variety gift store and we sell many different items. These books are going to sell and we'll become everyone's favorite place to buy the next big book from. You'll see."

"Okay," I say, deciding that I'd rather see her in this unusual good mood than burst her bubble by telling her how stupid this is. "I'll start putting them in inventory."

After the book-packed events of the morning, things settle down at the store. Mom hauls all the empty boxes out to the Dumpster, and I take some photos of our new bookshelf to post onto our social media sites. The books do look pretty cool on the shelf, and they have that delightful new book smell, and there's even some Young Adult books I've been wanting to read. But I can't help thinking this is a dumb idea.

By lunch time, Mom suggests that I should go out to the boardwalk and pass out the fliers she's made up for the store. They advertise our new book selection, and although I hate passing out fliers on the beach, I wouldn't mind getting some sun.

And getting away from my mom. She's being so happy and optimistic about these books and it's creeping me out. It's like she's a totally different person than she was just a few days ago when she was talking about getting a real job.

Luckily, the weather has cleared up from the storms over the last two days, and it's bright and sunny. I don a pair of oversized sunglasses and pull my hair into a messy bun and then I start handing out fliers to people. As I walk along the boardwalk, I pass by the video game store and think about asking them if I can leave some fliers on their front counter. I figure nerdy people play video games and so they might also read books, right? Or, at least the parents who buy games for their kids might be interested in books.

I approach the store and start to reach for the door handle when I see the large sign on the wall.

OUT OF BUSINESS

I stop, gazing up at the Games & More sign. It's been covered with a black tarp. The store is completely empty inside, all of the former shelves of video games are now collecting dust. When did this happen? It was only a week or so ago that I came in here to trade in some used DVDs for cash.

Then I see it. The sign of betrayal that is so obvious I can't believe I didn't think of it before. Jack Brown Properties is printed on the bottom of a sign that's been placed in the window.

He bought the video game store. And now he's coming after The Magpie. I grit my teeth and head back down the boardwalk. I'd been doing a half-assed job of passing out fliers before, but now I'm determined. I will give a flier to every book-loving person on this beach because I will not let Jack Brown buy our store from us. I don't care what it takes—I will sell every copy of those books my mom bought. Just thinking about earning enough money to forever be able to tell Jack Brown to piss off gives me motivation.

When all of my fliers are gone, I head back to the store and make copies of more. Mom had printed two fliers per page, but I shrink it down into four per page that way I can print twice as many.

While I'm cutting the papers into quarters, I call April.

"Please tell me you're not doing anything exciting," I say when she answers.

"That depends. Do you find laundry exciting?"

"Darn," I say with a fake sigh. "You're clearly having a very fun filled Saturday. So I guess I can't talk you into coming to the store and helping me out?"

She laughs. "What do you need help with?"

I explain the books and the fliers. "That sounds fun," she says. "I'll have my mom drop me off and I'll tell her to browse the books, too. She's a big reader."

My heart swells with gratitude. When April and her mom arrive, my mom immediately shows off the new books. April's mom and my mom have only met a few times, but they always act like they're close friends. We watch while they gush over books and when April's mom chooses three to purchase, my mom gives me a big smile.

April and I leave the moms to themselves, and we venture out onto the boardwalk. "So how's your tutoring going?" she asks.

I shrug. "I think I'm going to kick ass on my Chem test this Monday. I studied that stupid review website so many times that I've actually memorized things. Like…academic things."

"Awesome," she says. "I'm glad you're getting help but it sucks that I have to walk home alone two days a week."

"You could always hang out in the library and wait for me," I offer. That sounds epically boring, but April seems like the kind of person who wouldn't mind. She could get her homework done, because she's also the kind of person who does her homework.

"I would, but I don't want to be a third wheel," she says, turning a random grin on me.

"Huh?" I say, stopping to hand a flier to an elderly couple. "Hi there! The Magpie now has a selection of bestselling novels in stock. If you're interested, you can bring in this flier for an extra ten percent off!"

After they leave, I turn back to April. "There's no third wheel in tutoring," I say with a laugh. "But I have to warn you, you'll probably be bored to death."

She smirks. "Oh come on, Nat. You don't have to play dumb with me."

I stop mid-step and turn to her. "What are you talking about? I *am* dumb. That's why I have tutoring."

She rolls her eyes. "You also have a little *crush* on tutoring, I'd say."

Okay, now I'm really confused. "What are you talking about? I hate tutoring."

"Are you seriously not admitting it to yourself?" April shakes her head and hands a flier to the guy selling hot dogs from a cart. "You've been talking about Jonah nonstop, Nat. Like… every day since you started working with him."

"Uh yeah, because it sucks. I hate tutoring. You're the one I vent to every day."

She gives me a look and her intentions are unmistakable.

I put a hand on my hip. "You think I have a crush on Jonah?"

"You said it, not me," she says with a shrug.

I laugh. "I do not have a crush on him. He's like the hugest nerd on campus."

"Oh come on. He's totally cute," she says.

I feel my cheeks warming, even though I have no reason to be embarrassed. I guess I've never thought about it before but Jonah is kind of cute. I mean…in a nerd way.

"Absolutely not," I say instead. "He's not cute. He's just a guy. He's uptight and too smart and so nerdy it makes my head hurt."

"And he has a great smile and pretty eyes and you've said like three times that he smells good."

"I only said that because it's unusual for a teenage male to smell like anything other than body odor or cheap body spray."

I'm getting defensive, but I can't help myself. Jonah is a total dweeb. I don't like him. He's not cute. I could never stand dating someone who's so unbelievably nerdy. "April, you're losing your mind if you think I have a crush on the guy. He's just my tutor. He's not even my friend."

"But he could be more than that," she says in a singsong. She bats her eyelashes at me for emphasis. I shove her into a light pole.

11

MY LIFE HAS TAKEN A WEIRD TURN. IN JUST FORTY-EIGHT HOURS, things have happened that I would have never in a million years believed.

I studied chemistry so much I actually learned it.

The Magpie is now selling books and by that, I mean we're *selling* books. Twenty-four were sold on Saturday and at least that many more sold on Sunday. We make around seven dollars a book so that was a huge income boost.

Finally, and probably the most shocking turn of events ever —I can't stop thinking about Jonah.

I mean, *what?*

Why?

He's Jonah. He's an uptight nerd. He has perfectly styled hair and pressed, wrinkle free preppy outfits, and he organizes everything in such a way that means he's so unbelievably nerdy I want to die.

And of course, April had to run her stupid freshman mouth and put the idea in my head that I might have a crush on him. I don't.

I totally don't.

He's just like that stupid car wash jingle they play on the radio that gets stuck in your head for days at a time. Jonah Garza is just an annoying jingle. Not a crush.

On Monday, first period math class seems to fly by. I hadn't told Jonah this because I'd be embarrassed for him to realize just how much he's taught me, but I spent a little time last night on the school's math website. I studied the modules for the chapter we're currently learning in class, so that when Mrs. Mafi begins teaching it this morning, I'm already a little ahead of her. It makes more sense this way. I take notes and I pay attention, and the whole time I'm picturing Jonah in the back of my mind, that stupid lopsided grin on his face. He'd be proud of me if he knew this.

When the bell rings, I'm anxious to get to chemistry for our big test. Although I'd had a few nightmares this weekend of flunking the thing, I'm still pretty confident. The ChemXLabs website works so much better than filling out those stupid extra credit worksheets.

My backpack feels a hundred pounds heavier as I set it on the floor by my desk, knowing I still haven't worked on the extra credit. But I did study for this test and I think I'll ace it.

Mr. Greenstein passes out the tests, giving us detailed reminders that there is to be no talking until every student has finished. I hold my pencil tightly in my hand as I wait for my copy to land on my desk. Then I write my name at the top, take a deep breath, and get to work.

I'M CLUTCHING MY CHEMISTRY TEST IN MY HANDS THE NEXT DAY after school, trying to remain calm. Mr. Greenstein passed back all the graded papers at the end of second period, but I've had to wait until my tutoring session with Jonah to show him the results. Though I never see him in the hallways between classes,

I could have told him at lunch. I thought about it as I watched him sitting at a circular corner table in the far back of the cafeteria. Somehow, walking up to Jonah was just as intimidating as the idea of talking to Caleb at his lunch table. And that, of course, makes no sense because Caleb is my real crush. Jonah's just my tutor.

I shake the resulting emotions from my mind. There's no time to think about crushes and boys right now. It's officially Tuesday, which is tutoring day, and all I should focus on are my studies.

Yeah, right.

I stand at the entrance to the library, wanting to catch him the moment he walks in. Students rush past the library on their mad dash home, and none of the dark-haired guys who pass me are Jonah. He's always here before I am, and by the time the hallway has emptied out, I'm starting to wonder if he's ditching me today.

And then I get tapped on the shoulder.

I whirl around and find Jonah, who is somehow already in the library.

"Wha?" My mouth falls open. "I've been waiting for you. How did you get here?"

"I have computer lab last period," he says, tossing a thumb over his shoulder in the direction of the adjoining classrooms. "I just come in the back way."

"Oh." I don't know why, but I feel like an idiot. Standing around waiting for a guy is not something I like to do.

"My favorite color is blue," Jonah says. "I know it sounds lame because most people expect that a guy's favorite color is blue, but mine really is. It's the color of the sky and the ocean, and both of those things are very different shades of blue all the time." He reaches up and scratches his neck. "So that's why I like the color. It's beautiful in all of the shades."

"Okay…" I say, giving him a weird look as we walk to our table in the back of the room. "Why did you tell me that?"

"Because you got a ninety-three on your test," he says, giving me a lopsided smile as we walk. "I promised I'd tell you my favorite color once you passed a test."

I grin. The graded paper is still in my hands and I almost forgot about it when Jonah startled me just now with his quirky smile and sparkling eyes. I hold it up and show it to him. "How'd you see that so quickly?"

"I didn't," he admits, setting his messenger bag down in the chair next to him. "I checked in with your Chem teacher today after lunch. I was dying to know."

"And he just gave you my grades?" I say. "Just like that? I thought grades were private information."

He shrugs. "Mr. Greenstein knows I tutor you so I guess he was happy to show off your excellent grade. Great job, by the way. You might be my fastest learning student."

I sit at our table and rest my chin in my hand. "Does that mean I'll get a smiley face sticker on my page in your notebook?"

He rolls his eyes. "I don't use smiley face stickers."

"Well, you should. You can put it right next to that note you made about me."

He clears his throat, but he doesn't blush this time. It kind of annoys me that I can't get to him like I used to. "So what are we studying today, boss?"

Jonah leans back in his chair. "Anything you'd like."

I lift an eyebrow. "Really?"

He shrugs one shoulder. "You don't have any major tests coming up soon so we have some leeway on what to study. Is there any subject you're feeling the most behind in?"

"Yes," I say, reaching into my backpack. I pull out the folder with the stack of extra credit papers. "I'm very behind in the subject of Extra Credit." To prove my point, I let the folder drop onto the table with a thud.

Jonah chuckles. "Want to see how many you can knock out in the next two hours?"

My stomach twists into something that very much resembles butterflies as I watch Jonah. His little grin *is* pretty cute, not that I'd admit that to April. Or to myself. And there is something appealing about a clean cut guy who always smells nice. There's no caked on dirt underneath Jonah's fingernails, unlike just about every other guy ever. I have to resist the urge to lean in and close my eyes and inhale the nice scent of him.

I bite down hard on my tongue, trying to make the thoughts in my head go away. "I have a better idea," I say, putting my hand on top of the papers. "How about we split them and race and see who can do the most in two hours?"

I wink as I slide half of the papers toward him. "I have a feeling it'll be you."

"Nice try," he says, sliding them back. "How about you do your own extra credit work and I'll supervise and help as needed?"

I drop my lips into a pout. "That's no fun."

"I never said it would be," he says, meeting my gaze with a sultry one of his own.

I clear my throat. What am I thinking? Jonah isn't being sultry. He's being nice, that's all. Get it together, Natalie!

I swallow the lump in my throat and look down at the papers in front of me. "How about a compromise?" I say, trying to summon up that flirty energy I've had in the other times we've been together. Now, it's like it's all been taken away from me, and my body has been overrun with conflicting emotions. I exhale and try to act like I'm not battling thoughts of Jonah being cute.

"How about I do the worksheets, but after each one, you have to answer a fun question?"

He considers it for a moment. "Okay, but I have the right to veto a question."

"In which case I'd ask another one."

"Deal."

I can't hide my grin as I take the first worksheet and write my name at the top of it. The idea of learning more things about Jonah has me motivated to answer these stupid questions, some of which are pretty easy because they're from old lessons that I learned at the start of the school year when I was still attending class regularly. As I work, Jonah walks me through some of the harder problems, and I think about what question I'll ask him when this sheet is done. Finally, I place it at the bottom of the stack and look at him.

"Do you drive?" I ask.

"Yes," he says. His eyes meet mine and it sends a weird flurry of butteries through my stomach.

"What kind of car?" I ask.

He taps the paper in front of me. "If you want an answer, you have to do another worksheet."

I groan and shoot him a dirty look. "So mean to me..." I mutter under my breath.

"I am not mean to you," he says, sounding frustrated, but when I look over at him, he's smiling.

We do another worksheet and I get my answer. He drives a charcoal gray Lexus IS 250, which he says is not as cool as it sounds because it's seven years old and it used to be his dad's car before he upgraded.

I still think it sounds pretty cool. A Lexus? Mom's car is so old and crappy we don't even park next to a Lexus at the store because it's embarrassing by comparison.

We go on like this for the next hour, me blowing through the worksheet questions as fast as possible to get another answer out of him.

I learn that he has one dog named Rex, who is a German

Shephard they rescued from a shelter. He lives with his parents who are still married, and also his grandfather who moved in with them after having a stroke two years ago. His mother is from Mexico and his dad is from Washington. He has one little sister named Lola, and fourteen cousins who he grew up seeing almost every day.

I keep my questions light, never asking if he has a girlfriend even though I'm dying to know the answer. After each worksheet, the question dances around my tongue, but I refuse to say it out loud. Because if I do, that'll mean I might maybe care a little bit about Jonah's dating life, and I have to keep reminding myself that I don't. I don't care at all.

I like Caleb.

I like guys who aren't nerds.

Jonah is both a nerd and also not Caleb so I can't like him.

I finish another worksheet just before our two hours is up. Jonah grabs his bag and slings it over his shoulder as I pack up my stuff, shoving it into my backpack. I stand up and face him, noticing how he's just tall enough for me to be eye level with his lips. *He's the perfect height to give forehead kisses*, I think.

I quickly shove the thought away.

"You have one last question," Jonah says. "What'll it be?"

I can't help myself. I have to know.

"Was that pretty comment in your notebook about me?"

His eyes widen for a split second. "Yes," he says after a moment. "But I veto any follow up questions from now until forever."

He starts walking toward the door and I stand here a minute, watching him walk away. My chest aches in the weirdest way. It took a lot for him to admit that just now, even though we both already knew the answer from the moment I first saw his dog-eared comment on my appearance. And it takes even more for me to admit something to myself now.

I think I have a crush on him.

12

An entire week goes by with me doing a good job of keeping my new crush to myself. I'm still unsure about it, and wondering if I'm just suffering from delusional tutoring-induced emotions. Would I have liked Jonah if I never had to tutor with him?

Hell no.

So maybe all this studying is just rotting my brain.

The only good thing about being forced to go to tutoring and paying attention in class is that I'm not solely worried about the store anymore. I'm still stressed about it, and I still work there every day after school, but it's not the number one thing on my mind. Between the store, studying, and thinking about Jonah, there's barely any room for sleep.

But on Tuesday morning, I know my thoughts are about to spill over and come rushing out of my mouth because people can only keep these things to themselves for so long. The thing is, I need to make sure I control what I say instead of letting it escape accidentally. So I decide to tell April about my crush. She's the one who first pointed it out, after all. She is the best person to talk this through with me.

Only…as we're walking to school, I keep chickening out. I want to tell her, I do, but I can't make my mouth say the words. The thing is, even if I do have a crush on Jonah, I can't act on it. We are totally different people in very different social circles. He hangs out with the band nerds and fellow smart people and I keep to myself since I've lost most of my friends over the last year. I focus on the store and nothing else.

I don't even have time for a boyfriend.

"Are you okay?" April says as we approach the front doors of the school. "You look like you're going to puke."

"I might puke," I say and she jumps back. I laugh. "No, not literally…"

"So you're figuratively going to puke?" she says, giving me a look.

I shake my head and tuck into an empty part of the front lobby. "I need to tell you something, but only because I can't keep it to myself."

She lifts an eyebrow. "Okay, now I'm intrigued."

I take a deep breath and prepare to embarrass myself. "I think you're right. I think I might like Jonah."

"What!" she squeals. Her bright blue eyes seem to turn into glitter as she grins so big I can see all her teeth. "I knew it!"

"Shh!" I say, grabbing her hands before they can clap together excitedly. "The whole world doesn't need to know."

"But are you going to tell *him*?" she says, bouncing on the balls of her feet.

"No," I snap. Now I'm regretting telling her because this is all just too mortifying.

"Oh, come on," she says. She puts her hands on my shoulder and looks into my eyes like she's giving me some serious Yoda advice. "There's nothing wrong with liking Jonah."

At that very instant, the guy we're talking about walks up behind her. His eyes shine in greeting and his lips part like he's about to tell me good morning, just like he did the last couple of times I saw him before school started.

I shrug out of April's grip and I try to tell her to shut up before he hears anything. He's only a few feet away, getting closer with each step. But she's faster than I am.

"I know you said you'd never date a nerd like Jonah, but come on. He's cute."

"Morning," Jonah says quickly, glancing at me for a split second.

"Good morning," I say back, but he doesn't act like he heard me as he walks a little faster, his back to me now.

"Oh my God," April whisper-yells as she covers her mouth with her hands. "Do you think he heard me?"

My heart pounds so hard I can hear it in my skull. "I really, really hope not."

My throat goes dry as I walk to class. All of my muscles start to ache with worry and now it's all I can think about. Jonah was totally close enough to hear April call him a nerd. But it is loud in the hallways and maybe he wasn't paying attention.

Or maybe he was.

I have no idea, and the not knowing is driving me crazy. Because of this, I make a sixty on my Shakespearian quiz in English and I don't even hear when my History teacher calls my name three times in a row.

By the time the final bell rings, I don't know what to do or say when I see Jonah in tutoring. I decide to pretend that nothing happened and that everything is totally normal. After all, maybe he didn't hear it.

He was just passing by this morning. He was looking at me, so he probably didn't even pay attention to what anyone else was saying.

I've almost convinced myself that everything is okay until I get to our table in the library and Jonah's sitting there with his notebook open, his foot tapping impatiently on the floor.

"Let's get started," he says instead of a hello.

I swallow the lump in my throat and sit next to him, noticing that his chair is about six inches further away from mine than usual. He opens the history textbook to the chapter thirteen study guide.

"I'll quiz you on the vocab words," he says, never looking up at me.

My heart lodges in my throat. I can deny it all I want, but he definitely heard what April said this morning.

13

WE HAVE TO REORDER BOOKS TWO MORE TIMES. I CAN'T BELIEVE Mom's idea of selling books actually turned out to be profitable. As much as I like the idea of browsing a bookstore to find the perfect book for me, it turns out most people just like buying what's already labeled as a best seller. Some of our customers come into the store and grab the number one book without even reading the back summary to see if they'd like it. People are weird.

But I don't mind it at all if it helps the store.

I stand behind the counter working on my extra credit worksheets while Mom eats her dinner in the back room of The Magpie. Dinner tonight—and every night for the last week—has been peanut butter and jelly sandwiches. They're economical and cheap.

They also remind me of Jonah.

He'd told me they were his favorite snack food back when he was giving me answers for each paper I finished. Now, after suffering one very awkward tutoring session where he was all business and no small talk, I would give anything to go back to the way it used to be.

85

I debate telling him I'm sorry and just clearing the air about the whole thing. But knowing him, and how quiet he gets about stuff, he probably wouldn't even listen to me. He probably won't even admit that he heard the insult from April, although it's obvious that he did.

I think about leaving a note in his locker, or handing it to him in the hallway. I could apologize and say I want us to be friends.

But even that would just make the situation weirder. April thinks I should just ignore it and go back to the way things were. She says everyone eventually gets over stuff and he will be normal soon enough. But she doesn't sit in the tutoring session with me so she has no idea how impossible it would be to go back to my normal flirty self.

Just when he'd started opening up to me and joking around and telling me things, I'd gone and ruined it by talking about him to April. If boys and relationships were a grade in school, I'd be failing it for sure.

I spend all night thinking about what I should do. By the next morning, I've decided the best thing would be to apologize. Even if he doesn't want to hear it, and even if it's the most awkward thing I've ever done, Jonah deserves an apology.

Sure, he's nerdy and he's totally not the kind of guy I would date. But he's also a good person. I hate knowing that I've hurt his feelings.

I'm still trying to decide if I should apologize to him in class or after school during our tutoring session when I see him at lunch. He goes through the cafeteria line and grabs a burger and fries. I watch him carry his tray across the room to the circle table that's filled with his fellow nerd friends.

I decide that telling him now would be a good idea because then he'd have time to think about it before tutoring started. Maybe by then we'd be back to normal, or at least be able to pretend like we are.

I eat my food quickly and try to listen to whatever April is talking about. As soon as I'm done, I'm going to walk over there and ask to talk to Jonah alone really quick. I'll smile and I'll be friendly and say it's about my chemistry class.

I'm about to tell April that I'll be right back when I see a girl walk over to Jonah's table. She's short and petite with silky black hair and a pastel pink dress. I don't know her name, so she must be in a younger grade than me. She smiles at Jonah and he slides over, making room for her at the table. She opens the Diet Coke in her hand and slides a straw into the bottle's opening.

I run a hand through my hair and pretend to glance around the room, but really, I'm watching her every move. She touches his shoulder and laughs and steals some of his fries. He laughs back with her and together they chat with his friends.

She keeps doing this thing where she lays her head on his shoulder for a second. In the whole ten minutes I watch them, I don't think she stops smiling once.

"So I was thinking of watching Reign first and then Heartland because Reign has fewer seasons," April says. "What do you think?"

"Yeah, that's a good idea," I say, prying my eyes away from Jonah's table. An uneasy feeling settles into my stomach. Here I thought Jonah had spent the last two days hurting from the insult of being called a nerd. But really be probably didn't even care. Because, clearly, he has a girlfriend now. How could I have been so stupid? I should have listened to my gut in the first place and never allowed myself to like a guy who's in a totally opposite social circle.

I take a deep breath and tear my eyes away from his table. Jonah has his own life and I have mine. Our circles only connect briefly for two hours, two days a week. It is so not a big deal.

I take a deep breath and hold my head higher. Now that all the stupid crush stuff is over, I can go back to my normal life, like wondering if Caleb Brown will talk to me again in the hallways. I've only seen him once since that time Jonah interrupted us in the art hallway. He'd been walking with a group of football players and our eyes met from across the hall. He winked at me. And then he kept walking.

Still, I think. *Better than nothing.*

14

Some asshole vandalized our chalkboard last night. We usually bring it inside the store after closing up, but last night was Friday and the boardwalk had a live band playing so the place was more packed than usual. I'd had the genius idea to leave the sign outside near our store overnight so that all the people that were there seeing the band would walk past our sign and see that we sell books now. The best case scenario was that people who rarely come to the boardwalk would see the sign and remember our store and come back to buy books. I figured the worst thing that would happen is that people would just walk right by it, lost in their own world, and never see the sign.

I was wrong. The actual worst thing that could have happened would be the giant penis that now covers the board.

I heave a sigh and kneel down in front of it with a bottle of alcohol and some cotton balls. Luckily, I'm here early enough and it's Saturday morning so people like to sleep in. Maybe I can fix this before anyone sees it.

The penis is drawn in silver Sharpie, by the looks of it, and it spans the entire three-foot-tall chalkboard. I cover a cotton ball in alcohol and begin scrubbing at the lines. They come off with only a little effort, but when I'm finished, the alcohol has left a streak of perfectly clean black all over the board.

So the penis is still there in a way. I can't help but laugh a little at how stupid this is, and then I start scrubbing the entire thing until it's perfectly clean. I'm drenched in sweat by the time the board is finished, and the sun has risen and warmed up the beach.

I glance at the time on my cell phone and realize it's taken me two whole hours to clean off some asshole's idea of a funny joke. I wish we had a security camera on the store so I could find whoever did this and draw penises all over everything they love.

I head inside and find Mom behind the counter, playing on the computer. "All done?" she says, lifting an eyebrow at my appearance. I probably look like crap since I'm covered in sweat and I reek of rubbing alcohol.

I nod. "Where's the chalk markers?" She hands them to me and I go back outside, but not before chugging a cold bottle of water.

Mom has better decorative handwriting than I do, but I do my best to replace the words on the sign. I add an arrow at the bottom of it to point toward the store.

The boardwalk has filled up with people now, mostly beach-goers by the smell of the sunscreen in the air and the fact that people walk right past all the stores on their way to the ocean. I'm nearly finished with my sign when I hear a girl say, "*Seriously*, Jonah?"

My head whips up. Across the way, near the hot dog stand, is the petite girl from Jonah's lunch table. She's wearing cut off shorts and a black bikini top with no coverup so that her boobs are on display. And her hands are on her hips while she stares at Jonah.

My heart skips a beat. Seeing him outside of school is weirder than weird. He's wearing board shorts and flip flops.

And, well, I'm not going to say that the sight of his surprisingly muscular bare chest sends me falling to my ass on the board-walk, but I do have to reach over and grab the wall to steady myself. Maybe I've just been kneeling too long in front of this stupid sign and maybe that's why my knees are suddenly weak.

I'm partially hidden by the sign, and there's other people around, so I'm pretty sure they have no idea I'm here watching their private conversation. Which is good because I couldn't look away now, even if I wanted to.

Jonah's hair is either wet or gelled, because it's slicked to the side like usual, only it's a little messier than when he's in school. I try not to stare at his chest, but man. I had no idea he was packing such a hot body underneath those nerdy outfits he wears every day.

Here at the beach, he looks like a normal guy. With tanned skin and board shorts hanging low on his hips, I would swoon my ass off if a guy like him ever came into the store. It's amazing how different he looks, and I'm feeling like the worst person on earth right about now for judging him based on appearance.

Jonah called me pretty and I called him a nerd.

I cap the chalk marker in my hand. I should go back inside. But that girl's got her hand on her hip now as they move forward in line at the hot dog cart and she looks annoyed with Jonah. He says something I can't hear and then they order their food. He reaches into his back pocket and pulls out a wallet, handing some cash to Thamir, who owns the hot dog stand.

Watching him pay for her meal is all it takes to know they're a couple and that my fantasy of them being just friends is now just that—fiction.

Now I need to go inside. Watching them any longer just feels creepy and wrong. Over the next few hours, I work in the store and I tell myself a lot of things.

Like how I'm happy Jonah has a girlfriend.

And how I never liked him anyway.

And how both of those statements are a lie even though I won't admit it to myself.

The Magpie gets quite a lot of shoppers today, and although many of them are just browsing, many more purchase something. We sell enough books to make me think this might actually be a profitable venture, and I distract myself from thinking of Jonah by looking up new books to buy for the store.

It doesn't help much.

I'm not a superstitious person, and I don't believe in signs. One time sophomore year, my friend Tabby was asked to prom by this gorgeous senior guy. Only, two seconds after she'd said yes, some idiot threw a football in the hallway and it smacked her right in the face. She'd taken that as some kind of cosmic sign that she shouldn't go to prom. So she didn't.

I'm not the kind of person who believes in things like that, but when I look over at the clock on the computer at our front desk, the time is 11:11. I think back to being a kid and always making a wish at that time. They never came true. But I always wished anyway. Just like I do now.

I want to be friends with Jonah again.

And then, as if it's some kind of *actual* cosmic sign, I look out the window of the store and see Jonah's girlfriend storming down the boardwalk toward the parking lot. Even from here she looks pissed, her hands clenched into fists at her sides. I wait a few beats, but I don't see Jonah following behind her. Did he leave first? Or is he still on the beach?

I can't help my curiosity. I tell Mom I'm going to go grab us smoothies from the shop down the way and she eagerly hands me some cash because the smoothies are the greatest drink ever.

Then I'm out the door, heart pounding with curiosity. I walk slowly, scanning the area for the unexpectedly sexy guy who comes off as such a nerd at school. He's not on the boardwalk though, at least not where I can see. I venture a little further, down past the shops and to where the boardwalk ends and the beach begins.

And then I see him.

He's sitting on a large granite rock that separates the private part of the beach were people own beach houses and the public part. He's just staring off at the water, his toes in the sand.

I walk over to him. At first, I'm going to do this fake, "Oh hey! I didn't see you there! What a coincidence!" thing as I walk by, but the second I get close and he looks up and our eyes meet, I chicken out. I've never been a good actress.

"Hey," I say, walking over to the large boulder of granite he's using as a chair. It's about four feet tall and just as wide, cut into a jagged square shape by the industrial equipment that cut and hauled all of these to the beach years ago.

He doesn't say anything, but he gives me a half-hearted smile that doesn't reach his eyes.

"I saw your girlfriend leave," I say, staring at a streak of black in the rock instead of looking at him.

"What?"

I cringe a little. *Way to out yourself as a creepy stalker, Natalie.* "I'm at work," I say, trying to explain. "I saw you guys walk by earlier, and then I just saw her leave alone. She looked kind of pissed."

He stares at me, his eyes flitting from my left eye to my right one. He doesn't say anything so I get flustered and keep talking. "I'm not a stalker. I just—well the store—we have, like no customers most of the time. My mom owns The Magpie, in case you didn't know?" I point back toward the boardwalk. Sweat drips down my neck and it's not from the heat. "It's a gift shop," I explain, trying to remember if I ever told him about this. I think I did. He's still just looking at me though, not saying anything, and I can't stop talking. "It's a store and it's never busy so I was just sitting there bored staring out the window and I saw you guys."

I take a deep breath and stare out at the ocean. "Then I saw her leave and well—actually no, I wasn't, like, *stalking* you or anything. I was going to get smoothies for me and my mom and I saw her."

"Where's your smoothie?" he asks, squinting a little as he looks at me because the sun is so bright.

"I, uh, well I haven't gotten it yet. Um, I—" I stare down at my flip flops, now covered in sand. "I just wanted to see if you were okay."

"She must have looked really pissed," Jonah says, still watching me. For the first time since I've met him, he's actually staring at me, not glancing over and then looking away shyly. His stare feels like it's penetrating into my soul, like maybe he's trying to decide to forgive me or not.

I swallow. "What happened?"

He gives a little shrug and looks down at my hand, which is resting on the rock next to his.

"You don't have to tell me," I say, feeling like a total idiot for coming out here. "I guess I just wanted to find you and tell you I'm sorry for the other day. And, well, I'm sorry for everything. I wouldn't have been stupidly flirting and messing with you during tutoring if I knew you had a girlfriend. I was just mad that I even had to go to tutoring in the first place, so I tried to make it into a joke."

As the confession pours out of me, I realize it's all true. "Anyhow, I'm sorry, Jonah. I didn't know you have a girlfriend. I'll be nothing but professional at tutoring from now on."

"I don't have a girlfriend," he says. A gust of warm wind sends a strand of his hair falling into his face. "I have an ex-girlfriend, which is who you saw."

"Did you just break up?"

He shakes his head. "I broke up with her a couple months ago. She was just kind of a horrible person. Selfish. Rude." He shrugs and inhales a deep breath. "She ignored me for like a month and then she started texting and calling and saying she wanted to get back together."

I'm dying to know more. I want every single dirty detail, but I know better than to ask. Jonah shuts down easily and I should be grateful I've been told this much.

"That sounds hard," I say stupidly, just for something to say.

A tiny little bug lands on top of my finger on the rock and Jonah shoos it away. "I was open to trying to get back together, but I told her things had to be different. She couldn't be so rude all the time. She acted like she agreed with me, but every time we hang out, it's the same old stuff."

He kicks his foot and sends a wave of hand skittering across the shore. "Last week she makes this big deal about telling all our friends that we're not dating officially and that we're just *hanging out*. She doesn't want me to hold her hand but she wants to be doted on. And then we come here and I don't immediately offer to buy her food and she gets pissed. Call me crazy, but if we aren't officially dating, why should I buy her food?"

"You shouldn't," I say.

He sighs and runs a hand through his hair, which only makes more of it flip over to the side. I bite the inside of my lip because right now the boy looks like a freaking cologne model about to do a beach themed photoshoot.

"I don't even know what she got pissed about just now," he says. "But she got mad and stormed off. She wants me to chase after her because she thinks that kind of drama is romantic or some crap."

"No, that kind of drama is screwed up," I say.

He grins. "Glad I'm not the only one who thinks that. I just want a real relationship that's not based on these freaking games."

"So dump her," I say. "You shouldn't waste your time on a drama queen like that. Quit answering her calls and let her find some other poor guy to screw with."

He looks up at me again, and this time there's a sadness in his eyes. "I can't do that."

"What? Why?"

"Because, *Natalie*," he says, saying my name like I'm a child. "Guys like me have to take what we can get. It's not like there's a line of girls waiting around to date a pathetic nerd. You of all people should know that."

15

April covers her face with her hands. She shakes her head slowly and I feel her embarrassment for me just as strongly as I feel the morning breeze in my hair. "Oh my God," she says, uncovering her eyes. She's still shaking her head. She looks down at the sidewalk and kicks a rock. "Oh my God."

"Is that all you have to say?" We come to a stop at the intersection before school and I give her a look. "I could use a little... I don't know, support."

She barks out a laugh. "Natalie, I don't know. That's just..." She shakes her head quickly. "So sad. And cringey. And—"

"Okay, enough." I hold up my hand to silence her. "I have to stop telling you these embarrassing things because you only make me feel worse, not better."

"I'm sorry, Nat." April takes a deep breath. "I am here for you. What can I do?"

A school bus drives by and then we cross the road onto school property. It's Monday morning and I've just told her what happened on the beach with Jonah this weekend.

I sigh and try to push out the memory of Jonah's face when he called me on my nerd comment. "Can you invent a time machine?"

I ask her. I try to smile but it doesn't really work. "Then I could go back in time and never let him hear you call him a nerd."

"Hey, *you* called him a nerd!" she says, pointing a finger at me.

"Yeah, but you said what I said out loud and he heard it."

She rolls her eyes. "Semantics!"

I grab my backpack straps and stare at the cracked sidewalk as we make our way to the school. Today is one thing, but tomorrow I have tutoring with Jonah and I just don't know how I can handle it. I feel so awful.

"So nothing happened after he said that?" April says. "He didn't like… try to lighten the mood or anything?"

I shake my head. "He was like, 'You of all people should know that' and then he ran a hand through his hair and walked off."

April's eyes go big. "You should have said something."

"I know!" My voice is so loud it makes two guys look over at us. I roll my eyes and keep walking. "Trust me, I know," I tell April. "I feel stupid. I mean, here I am crushing on him and he totally hates me now."

"So what did you say his ex-girlfriend looks like?" she asks.

"Short, dark hair, olive skin," I say with a sigh. "Prettier than I'd like to admit. If she were ugly, maybe I wouldn't care as much."

"She's an *ex*," April says. "You can fix this."

I shake my head. "I don't think I can. He hates me now. And it's for the best because what was I even thinking?" I scrunch up my face and try very hard to believe what I'm saying. Deep down I know the words are true. "I don't like Jonah. It was just a momentary lapse of judgement."

"Okay," April nods sharply as if she's also going to lie to herself in order to believe what I've just said. "See you at lunch?"

"Yep."

April turns down the hallway with all the freshman lockers and I keep walking toward my first period class. April likes to stop at her locker between every class, but I never use mine. I'm lazy and prefer to lug my backpack around everywhere.

As I near the math hallway, someone calls my name. I turn around and see the guy I've truly been crushing on jog up to me. My heart skips a beat.

Caleb is wearing distressed dark wash jeans that hug his muscular thighs in all the right places. His shirt is white and also tight-fitting, showing off the bulging muscles he works hard on in the gym. His physique is bigger and bulkier than Jonah's, but you can expect that from a jock.

Oh my God, am I still thinking about Jonah?

I smile and try to clear my thoughts as Caleb gives me this smirk that's so hot it could melt the lockers he leans up against now. "Hey," he says as his smirk turns into a grin. "Haven't seen you in a while."

"Well, you know how much I love the math hallway," I say, gesturing to our surroundings. "If you need me, I'm usually here."

He laughs even though my joke wasn't that funny. "So, Natalie—" He reaches forward and pokes me in the shoulder and I have no idea why my insides turn to goo at just a simple poke. "I was thinking we should hang out this Friday."

"Yeah," I say entirely too eagerly, which makes heat rise in my cheeks. I clear my throat. "Yeah, that's cool. Any reason why?" I have to ask because I can't be sure what's going on here. My heart is dying for a date with Caleb Brown, but what if this turns into some stupid misunderstanding and he really wants me to meet up with him for non-romantic reasons?

He shrugs and leans against the lockers in this way that makes him even sexier, if that's possible. "Just thought we could hang out," he says, reaching out and letting his fingers slide down my arm. Goosebumps prickle along my skin. "You seem like a cool girl."

Oh my God oh my God oh my God.

It's a date.

It's a *date,* date. Not a misunderstanding.

Be. Cool.

I draw in a breath slowly and consider my words before I let them fall out of my mouth. I will not be that stupidly eager girl who throws herself at him. I won't be lame. I'll be sexy and mysterious and make him want more.

"You said *this* Friday?"

He nods, his blue eyes peering into mine in a way that reminds me of that shaggy haired boy he used to be, not the clean cut short haired jock he is now.

"Let me guess, hopscotch and bicycle races like in the old days?"

He looks confused for a minute and then he smiles. "Man, that was a long time ago. It's weird that we knew each other as kids."

"Well, we have lived in the same town and gone to the same school our whole lives."

"And our parents own businesses on the boardwalk," he says. "We practically lived there as kids."

I nod. Back when Jack Brown wasn't a threat to my mom's business.

"Unfortunately," Caleb says, brushing my arm again, "I wasn't planning on bike races this time. You'll have to settle for hanging out with me without a bike."

It takes everything I have not to jump up and down with excitement. "Sure," I say with a casual nod. "Friday sounds fun."

"Cool," he says with a grin. "Give me your phone."

I hand it over and he types in his number then presses the call button before handing it back to me. "I'll text you later," he says. His fingers touch mine when he hands me my phone and it sends a jolt of something through my body. Lust? Desire?

I don't know, but I do know I want more of it.

THE NEXT DAY, APRIL AND I HAVEN'T FOUND ANYTHING ELSE TO talk about besides my upcoming date with Caleb. We gushed about it at lunch yesterday, and then on the walk home from school, and then on the walk to school today, and now it's lunch time and we're back at it. That's the best part of hanging out with a freshman—they don't pretend to be too cool to talk about boys. My old friends would have never cared about this.

I dunk a fry into nacho cheese sauce and gaze across the cafeteria toward the athletes' table.

"You should go sit with him," April says, nudging me in the arm.

"No way." I shake my head and reach for another fry. "He hasn't even talked to me since." As if on impulse, I glance down at my phone on the cafeteria table in front of me. After I saved Caleb's number in my phone, I've spent pretty much every second of my life hoping he'll text me. But he hasn't. It's only been one day though, and guys are notorious for making girls wait three days.

"He asked you out so he obviously likes you," April says. "Go say hi."

"No way. He's sitting with his friends and I'm not going to be the girl who's clingy and annoying on day one. You have to slowly win over the friends."

"Screw the friends! A hot guy has a date with you on Friday. Go flirt with him so you'll be less nervous on the actual date!" April gives me this exaggerated wink that makes me laugh.

"I'm not doing it," I say with an adamant shake of my head. "I'm going to be the cool mysterious chick who he has to chase."

She rolls her eyes. "Whatev."

"So in other news," I say as my heart starts to beat a little faster. "I still haven't looked at it."

"At what?" April says with her mouth full of food.

"*It*," I say, tapping my binder on the table.

"Oooh," she says. "This semester's progress report."

I reach for the paper, which is folded in half and stapled together. That's how our homeroom teacher passes them out each semester so the grades are somewhat private. I've had mine for a few hours now and I'm too scared to look. I take out the paper and slide my finger under the staple, ripping it open.

"You can do it!" April says.

"It's only been a couple of weeks. My grades won't be much higher," I say, chewing on my lip. We haven't had enough grades yet to even out my average, but I'm still hopeful that I might be passing all of my classes.

With a deep breath, I open the paper.

Last time I was failing math, chemistry, and history.

This time I'm failing math, chemistry, and history.

My shoulders fall.

"It's not so bad," April says as she leans over my shoulder to see the grades. "You had thirties and forties and now you're in the sixties."

"Still not passing," I say, folding the paper back up. I don't know what I was expecting. Having a thirty-six in math class takes longer than two weeks to turn into a C or a B. A thirty-six is like…a triple F.

"You're being too hard on yourself," April says sweetly. "You're really close to passing and there's still two and a half months of school left."

"Yeah, I know." Without thinking about it, I look up at Jonah's table.

He's looking right at me.

Chills scatter across my arms as we make eye contact. I want to smile or wave at him, or show him my grades since I know he'd be interested. But I am frozen with shame for what I called him, and how badly I've hurt his feelings, so I don't do anything.

His ex-girlfriend grabs his arm and tugs his attention away from me. She says something to him and then runs her hands through his hair, shaping it into a bigger version of a side-sweep. Then she cups his cheeks in her hand and says something that makes her laugh.

I look back at my food, wishing the sight of them together didn't send a wide array of emotions through my heart. He deserves someone better than her. He also deserves someone better than me. He just deserves…better.

I shove my food away, unable to eat anymore with the turmoil that's bubbling up in my stomach. April fills the silence with stories from her Home Ec. class, and I shove my progress report deep in my backpack so I don't have to look at it anymore.

I try to go back to being excited for my date on Friday, but knowing I'll have to see Jonah after school today makes me feel sick to my stomach.

Just before the final bell rings, I take out my phone and look up Jonah's number. He'd given it to me on our first day of tutorials in case I ever needed to reach him. So far, we haven't texted at all, but I send him one now.

Me: Sorry I can't make tutoring today. Something came up

Jonah: no prob. See you Thursday

Well, I think, as I stare at the first new text I've had all day. *At least he doesn't seem to mind.*

16

IF THE HUMAN BRAIN IS SUPPOSED TO BE THIS GLORIOUS ORGAN capable of sending a man to the moon and curing smallpox, why can't my mind work properly? All it does is think about my date with Caleb. Before that, all it did was think about Jonah. And then the store.

The phrase "one track mind" applies here, I think. Maybe it's the teenage hormones. Maybe I'm just broken. But as I sit in class trying to work on these extra credit assignments, my hand just hovers the pencil over the first problem. It doesn't write anything. I read the words over and over but they don't make any sense because I'm not focusing. My mind is a train stuck on one track and that track is Caleb Brown.

In the hallways between classes, I can barely function like a normal human because I'm constantly wondering if he'll find me again, lean against the lockers and chat with me. Or better, if he'll walk with me to my next class. I close my eyes and think of the smell of him, how it's a little overpowering but still good.

Then it makes me think of Jonah and how he smells better. I grit my teeth and try to ignore that. Jonah may smell better, but

Caleb is popular, handsome, and he likes me. We're going on a date. That is all that matters.

I don't see him all day, except for during lunch where he's at his normal table. April encourages me to go say hello, but that would be like telling a deer to go say "hi" to a group of starving lions. I'm not that stupid.

Disappointment stings, but I try not to think about it. Maybe this is protocol for going on dates. You don't really hang out until after the date. Too bad that's three days away.

On Wednesday, things aren't any better. April can probably tell that I'm feeling weird because she talks the entire time we walk to school and then she talks all through lunch, and she texts me jokes and stupid photos while I'm in class to make me feel better. But another day of being totally ignored by Caleb really gets to me and I'm starting to question if he ever asked me out or not. Maybe I tripped and fell in the hallway that day, banging my head on the wall. Maybe I was hallucinating that Caleb walked up being all unbelievably sexy and leaned against the lockers and asked me out for Friday. Maybe it was all just a dream.

I know that's mostly just the paranoid part of my brain talking, because there's no way I could have hallucinated so realistically, but it's enough to keep me from approaching Caleb myself. Because after all, he asked me on a date and then hasn't sought me out again. Maybe I *did* imagine it.

And since my one track mind has been remarkably stuck on thoughts of Caleb, I text Jonah again telling him I can't make tutoring on Thursday. He doesn't reply right away like he did last time I blew him off, and it gets me worried that maybe he's in the library waiting on me. April and I have nearly walked all the way home when he finally writes back.

Jonah: okay

Single word texts are the worst. I stare at my phone as I walk into my house and toss my backpack on the couch. Tomorrow is my date with Caleb, so I should spend today working on as much extra credit worksheets as humanly possible for the next hour until I head to the store and give Mom a break from work.

But extra credit work is what someone responsible would do. I can't seem to find the energy. I keep staring at my phone, wishing Jonah had said something—anything—else. I don't know why. It makes no sense, but I want him to talk to me. I want us to feel like we're back to normal so I can go back to tutoring and actually learn something.

I make a PB&J sandwich and eat it quickly while staring at my phone. Finally, I break. I have to say something.

Me: Don't worry about the missed tutoring. I'll just go to Saturday detention to make up my time.

Jonah: No need…I signed in for both of us today and told the librarian we were studying outside.

I stare at the phone, nearly choking on my Diet Coke.

Me: You covered for me?

Jonah: Of course. That's why I'm such a good tutor.

Me: kind of sounds like you're a terrible tutor… ;-)

Jonah: Okay, terrible tutor but good friend.

My heart warms and I read his texts over again to make sure I didn't interpret them wrong. He lied to the school administration so that I'd still be counted as present for detention. I don't have to make up an additional day because of him. He called himself my friend.

I can't get the stupid grin off my face until Friday morning, when I wake up nervous about my date tonight. Even though it won't take place until after school, I still agonize over what to wear from my closet, and it makes me ten minutes late to meet with April in the morning. I've decided on a pair of skinny jeans, black converse, and a black V-neck tee that somehow makes my boobs look bigger while simultaneously just being a plain shirt that makes it look like I'm not trying.

But I'm so trying.

I just know this is the day that Caleb will finally come talk to me in class. I take my time in the hallways, lingering around so that I'm easy to spot should he be looking for me.

But he never is.

Or maybe he never finds me.

The day blows by in a way that is both fast and slow. My classes seem to take forever, but before I know it, the final bell has rung and I'm meeting April after school to walk home. I look all around for Caleb in the parking lot. If he's going to offer to give us a ride again, it'd be today, right?

"You freaking out about your date?" April says the moment she finds me waiting at our usual spot.

"Is it that obvious?" I ask.

She shrugs as she falls into step with me. "It's a big deal, dating a popular jock. I'd be freaking out, too."

"I'm starting to wonder if I just imagined it," I say with a sigh as I give up on scouting the parking lot. "Why would a guy ask me out one day and then not talk to me for the rest of the week?"

"Because he's nervous?" April says.

I bark out a laugh. "Yeah right. Caleb Brown nervous of dating me? Never in a million years."

"Give yourself some credit," she says. "He asked you out after all. That's something."

I take a deep breath and try to have some confidence. "I guess so."

As much as I try to fight it, the tears start to pour from my eyes at 8:15. It's been one hell of a Friday night, and any confidence I tried to have earlier today has been shattered, ripped, and torn until there's absolutely nothing remaining.

Caleb hasn't called me. Hasn't texted me. Hasn't sent a carrier pigeon.

I left Mom to work the store by herself tonight while I got ready for my date, only to realize that the date wasn't happening. Mom closed up at six and came back home, ate dinner, and started watching a movie with a glass of wine, all while I've been sitting here on my bed staring out the window. I guess I hoped that maybe Caleb would just show up for our date without calling first. It could happen.

Of course it didn't.

He forgot.

Or maybe he never meant it.

Maybe it really was a hallucination.

Whatever the case, I'm crying now. Hot tears roll down my cheeks, splashing on the silk tank top I'd put on for a date that isn't happening. I know it's messing up my makeup but there's no point in caring about that now. I've been stood up.

My phone buzzes a few minutes later. Probably April, wondering how the date is going. My cheeks burn as I think about how I'll tell her. This is so embarrassing.

When I check the text, it's not from April.

Caleb: you ready?

I swallow and quickly wipe away my tears. It's 8:30 at night, but it's still technically Friday. My heart pounds as I think about what to write back. Did he forget about me and then remember last minute? Or is going out this late just what the cool kids do?

Me: For what?

Caleb: ha ha. Be there to pick you up in five mins

I jump out of bed. Maybe this is normal. Maybe the popular jocks always go out on dates at 8:30 p.m. on Fridays. Was I just feeling sorry for myself for nothing? Who cares! There's no freaking time to think about this.

I rip off my tear-soaked silk shirt and put on another one, a dark blue tight fitting shirt that shows a little cleavage. I run to the bathroom and touch up my makeup and then grab my purse and wait by the door.

Mom looks over at me, pausing her movie. "You're still here? I thought you had a date."

"I'm about to leave," I say, throwing my hair over my shoulder. It's important to act casual now because if Mom suspects that I've just been upstairs crying, she'll probably want to talk about it. "The movie starts late," I explain with a smile even though I have no idea what we're doing tonight. The movies are a possible option, though, and they do have late movies. Maybe I was worried for nothing.

"Well don't invite him in," Mom says, tugging her bathrobe closer around her chest. "I'm not fit for company."

Fine by me, I think. Meeting the parents is always so awkward. A few minutes later, I see headlights pull into our driveway, so I tell Mom bye and dash outside. Caleb grins at me from the driver's side of his truck. Some of the knots in my stomach fade away. I don't know what I was so worried about.

I reach for the passenger door handle just as the door pops open on its own.

Then I realize it wasn't accidental—someone from the back-seat leaned forward and opened it. "Hi," I say as I climb into the car. There are two football players in the backseat, both smelling like body wash and liquor.

"Sup, little mama?" one of them says.

I turn to Caleb, a questioning look in the smile I give him. "Natalie, these idiots are Jeremiah and JT. Don't let them hit on you, you're with me tonight."

His grin warms me up inside and I want to make all of the truck's air vents blow on my face to cool me down. So we're not alone. That's okay. He's just claimed me as his, which is kind of hot.

I buckle up and tell myself to act cool as he pulls out of the driveway and heads toward downtown Sterling.

"You have a good week?" he asks me. I nod. He nods back. "Cool."

We go to the arcade, which is like part restaurant, part bar, part arcade games. There's five more guys from the team there and it seems like they've already been drinking despite not being old enough to order anything at the bar.

Caleb introduces me to the guys and then promptly gets into a battle of air hockey with one of them, leaving me standing awkward and alone.

It goes on like this all night. Caleb and his friends play arcade games, loudly cheering and messing with each other. I play a few games just to fit in, but I'm not having fun. This is not a date. I don't even know what this is.

I don't really have a curfew since I'm never out very late and my mom is pretty relaxed about stuff like that, but when it's nearly midnight, I decide to make my escape from this crappy night.

"Hey," I say, tugging on Caleb's arm. He's focused on the intense game of foosball in front of him because he's supposed to play whoever wins this round.

"You hungry?" he says, putting an arm on my lower back. He glances at me for just a second and then looks back at the game. That's how it's been all night. The only time we talk is if he's asking if I want something. He did buy me a drink and some cheese fries earlier, but then he hung out with his friends instead of eating with me.

I shake my head. "It's getting late. I think I'll head home."

"I drove you," he says, dipping his head as he grins at me. "You can't get home without me."

"Oh...um..." Why hadn't I thought of that? "I'll just call someone to get me," I say. "No big deal."

"Absolutely not," Caleb says. He bops me on the nose with his finger. "Let's go."

Then he takes my hand and leads me through the arcade. I

get this thrill of nerves in my stomach at the feeling of his hand on mine. Besides a few hand touches on my back, this is all the attention I've gotten from him tonight. We round the corner of a large video game and suddenly he's pulling me into a darkened area that leads to the employee breakroom.

"Been meaning to do this all night," he says, grabbing my face in his hands.

"Do what?" I say stupidly.

That's when he kisses me.

17

CALEB'S LIPS ARE SOFT AND TASTE LIKE THE DR. PEPPER HE DRANK earlier. There's a hint of stubble on his jaw that scratches against my cheek as he kisses me. I feel it prickling my skin in this delightful way and I'm partially wondering why my brain thinks all these things during my first kiss with the guy I like, and I'm partially freaking out because Caleb Brown is kissing me.

He's a rough kisser, pressing his lips to mine as if he's determined to prove something. I close my eyes and kiss him back, using my limited knowledge on how to do this. His hands are on my sides, and then my back presses against the wall that smells a little like cotton candy.

When he pulls back for air, he gives me this devilish grin. "I've waited all night to do that."

I'm still stunned from the kiss, so I don't say anything.

Caleb's tongue flicks across his bottom lip and then he leans forward, slowly moving toward me. My stomach flutters at his nearness, and then his lips are on mine, soft this time. His hand slides down my waist and stays there, resting just above the waistband of my jeans. "You want to go back to my house for a little bit? My parents aren't home."

My breath hitches. I'm not an idiot and I know what he means. As much as I like him, I definitely want to keep making out behind a wall of arcade games. But I don't want to go back to his house with him alone…and do the things that boys expect when you're alone.

"Um," I say, suddenly more nervous than I've ever been in my life. If I say no, he won't like me anymore.

"Dude!" Jeremiah shoves Caleb's shoulder. "There you are! I've been looking everywhere."

"What's up, man?" Caleb asks, straightening and dropping his hold on me.

"I need a ride home," Jeremiah says, looking at his cell phone. "Like, now. My mom's pissed about something, I don't know."

Caleb looks at me and frowns. "Looks like we have to leave anyway."

Saved by the drunken jock, I think as I look at the time on my watch. "Actually, I should probably get back too."

"Okay," he says, wrapping an arm around my shoulders. I breathe a sigh of relief because he doesn't seem upset that I've managed to slip out of his offer to go back to his house.

Jeremiah reeks of alcohol which flows up from the backseat of Caleb's truck and stings my nose. He spends the whole time talking about how he's a better air hockey player than anyone at the arcade. Caleb says that my house is closer, so he takes me home first, and I'm kind of grateful for it. This whole night has been one confusing weird mess. First, Caleb ignores me all week and then he ignores me most of the night until he randomly decides to kiss me. I don't know what to make of that. I can't wait to get into my bed and process everything that's happened.

When he pulls into my driveway, he leans over and kisses me on the lips. "Have a good night," he says, winking at me.

"You too." I smile and then get out of the car. He backs out of my driveway before I've made it to the door and I tell myself I don't care that he's not exactly a polite gentleman who walks me to my door. I'm pretty sure guys don't even do that stuff anymore.

I guess I should know better by now, but it's a little disappointing when he doesn't text me for the rest of the night. As the weekend comes and goes, I spend all of my time at The Magpie trying to drum up customers between staring at my phone hoping for a text. But I'm starting to think that Caleb Brown is just the kind of guy who never uses a cell phone. Or maybe he just doesn't use it to talk to me.

MY MONDAY MORNING WALK TO FIRST PERIOD IS A BLUR. I'M purposely trying not to pay attention to the faces in the hallway. Caleb hasn't texted me or otherwise acknowledged that I exist in any way, so I'd prefer to do the same for him. I don't want to look for him. I don't want to think about him.

When someone walks up a little too close to me, I'm about to ignore them as well until I recognize the soapy scent of Jonah.

"Good morning," he says, flashing me a smile.

"Hey." I hate that he's giving me that cute smile when we're supposed to just be friends. It makes me think of those few days when I thought I had a crush on him.

"Just came by to wish you good luck on your history exam."

"My what?" I come to a dead stop in the middle of the hallway. "Is that today?"

His hand slides down the strap of his messenger bag and he nods. "You have Mrs. Lapin fifth period, right? She's giving the exam to all of her senior classes today."

I sigh and toss my head back, muttering a curse under my

breath as I stare at the ceiling. "I completely forgot. I was supposed to study this weekend."

Jonah's lips slide to the side of his mouth, and I can practically hear his thoughts about how if I'd just been at tutorials last week we could have studied for it. "I can study with you at lunch, if you'd like."

"Really?" The flash of excitement I get is quickly overshadowed by my history with Jonah. "Wait, I can't make you sacrifice your lunch for me."

"Sure you can," he says with a shrug. "Plus, I'm offering. I don't mind."

"What about your girlfriend?"

"Tutoring comes first," he says, glancing down the hallway instead of looking at me. "If you fail this test, it looks bad on me so I'm really doing this for myself too, if it makes you feel better."

"That does make me feel better." I don't really hear the words I'm saying because I'm struggling against the pain my chest. Jonah's reply is not what I wanted to hear. I wanted him to say something like, *"Girlfriend? What girlfriend? The only girl I care about is you."*

But that stuff only happens in fantasy worlds, I guess.

"Thanks," I say, trying to smile. "Let's meet at lunch."

"Meet me by the recycling?" he says, glancing at me quickly before looking down at his phone, even though the screen is off.

"Sure thing."

I do my best to pay attention in math, chemistry, and English classes because I know I'll get to study for the history exam during lunch. Now that I've been actually working on my grades, it turns out paying attention to the lesson as it's taught is much easier for me. I actually understand what's going on now that I'm somewhat caught up in class. Still, that lingering exam in History class is nagging at me and I wish I'd remembered to study for it this past weekend.

Anger replaces my regret and I could kick myself for wasting so much precious time thinking about Caleb. I think it's pretty obvious he doesn't even like me that much. If anyone else had told me that a guy treated them so pathetically on their first date, I would tell her to leave him. Yet here I am, still wishing he'd text me.

Why am I so pathetic? I shove down the feelings that I'm still not over my little crush on Jonah and that it's making me focus on Caleb too much. I miss the days when I didn't really care about any guy. When my life was composed of worrying about the store and skipping school.

At lunch, Jonah is waiting for me at the recycle bins that are next to the doors to the cafeteria. I've already texted April to tell her I won't be in lunch, but I still feel slightly bad about ditching her.

"I secured a study room for us," Jonah says, flashing me a grin as he walks out of the cafeteria. "Mr. Hawkins said the room across from his is empty so it's all ours for the day."

"Can I come here every day during lunch?" I say, thinking how great it would be to avoid looking over at other tables and seeing people I don't want to see, like Jonah's girlfriend.

"Doubt it," he says, oblivious to my thoughts.

The classroom is empty except for rows of desks. We sit at the back and Jonah pulls his desk toward mine so that we're facing each other. "I'll quiz you," he says, pulling out his history textbook and opening it to the chapter about the Civil War.

I'm trying to decide if Jonah has suddenly gotten cuter or if I'm just used to his nerdy polo shirt and khakis by now. In a way, it's almost sexy how he doesn't care if he's dressed like a middle aged businessman instead of a teenage boy. My thoughts float back to seeing him on the beach, shirtless in flip-flops. He looked like his age there. My cheeks redden.

Jonah asks another history question and I answer it, my voice a little raspy. I clear my throat and tell myself to stop thinking about what he looks like without his shirt on. This history exam is important. I have to focus.

"This was fun," I say as the lunch period is almost over. "I missed studying with you last week."

"I missed you too," he says, closing up his textbook and putting it in his messenger bag. My eyes widen. Did he mean to say those exact words—he missed me—or did he mean he missed our studying?

"Look, Jonah..." I swallow the lump in my throat and take courage from the fact that we're all alone in here. "I'm really sorry about that day...when you heard April talking about you..."

His bottom lip pulls under his teeth and he looks at the desk. "It's fine, Nat."

"No...it's not... I mean, I don't know what all you heard, but —" I take a deep breath even though my cheeks are burning and I feel like an asshole and this is so embarrassing. Jonah is a good guy and I can't stand the thought of him going around life thinking he's a nerd, or someone unattractive. I have to make this right. I look up at him and he's watching me, a curious expression on his face.

"When we first started tutoring together I was just mad about it. I didn't want a tutor and I didn't want to go, so I bitched about it to April. I called you some unflattering names, but I would have said that about anyone because I was mad about the tutoring."

He watches me, his expression softening. I continue, "So then we were talking about you, and I was saying you're not so bad and she repeated what I'd called you, and that's the part you overheard. But it's not true, Jonah. I didn't mean it. You could have been any other student tutor and I would have said the same thing."

I can't bring myself to say the word *nerd*, so I dance around it. "I'm so sorry, Jonah."

He stares at his fingers for a moment, pressing them to the desk. "It's fine, Natalie. You don't have to explain."

"But I do. I have to apologize. I don't want you thinking you're anything less than amazing, because you are."

His lips turn up a little in the corners. "Thanks," he says, meeting my eyes. "I broke up with Lara, by the way."

"Your girlfriend?"

"Ex." He shrugs. "She's kind of a bitch. After we talked that day at the beach, I got to thinking that I'd rather just be alone than be with someone like her."

I realize I'm smiling in this huge, giddy way, and I quickly make my face go back to normal. "That's good. I'm proud of you. You deserve so much better than her."

"Hopefully," he says. The bell rings and he stands. "Good luck on your test. I think you're going to do great."

It feels like a ton of weight has been lifted from our friendship now that we've gotten this talk over with. I'm happy Jonah ditched that girl and I'm glad I got to apologize for calling him a nerd. I can't believe it, but I'm actually looking forward to tutoring this week.

"Walk me to history class?" I say as we leave the empty classroom. "You can quiz me all the way there."

He grins and shoves his hands in his pockets. "I'd love to."

18

Mrs. Lapin reuses the same tests from class to class, so instead of letting us write on them, she has us number one through thirty on a piece of our own paper and then we fill in our multiple choice answer. The cool thing about this way of testing is that she can grade our tests instantly by putting our answer sheet up against her master key.

The bad thing? She can grade it instantly.

I walk up to her desk to turn in my exam and she smiles at me, then puts my paper next to her answer key. I want to turn around and run back to my desk as fast as my legs will take me, but most kids stand around and wait to see their grade. I force my feet to stay planted near her desk and I wince when she marks one wrong right at the start. A few seconds go by and she makes another x and then another. I look away, focusing on the date she's written on the dry erase board.

"Not bad," she says a few seconds later. She hands my paper back and I look down, seeing my grade written in red pen and circled at the top right corner.

Relief washes over me. An eighty-nine. That's not failing. In fact, that's almost an A. I can't help but grin as I take my paper back to my desk. The last minute studying paid off.

I snap a photo of my grade and text it to Jonah.

Me: I couldn't have done this without you!

He responds by sending about fifty smiling face emojis. For the first time since I was a young and stupid high school freshman, college feels like it might actually be attainable. And I owe it all to my ex stepdad's new wife who forced me to get tutored. Go figure.

JONAH SLAPS SOMETHING ON MY HAND WHEN I WALK INTO tutoring on Tuesday afternoon. I look down and see it's a pink sparkly sticker of a unicorn that takes up almost my entire hand.

"Are you a big fan of unicorns?" I say as I sit next to him at our usual table.

"My little sister loves them," he says, pulling out his notebook. "My parents give her a sticker to celebrate any accomplishment she attains."

I hold my arm up to examine the sticker. "So why are you giving me one?"

"She said you should get one for your fantastic grade on the history test."

I give him a curious look and his cheeks flush a deep and glorious shade of red. "You told your little sister about my grade?" I ask, leaning forward. "When would that ever come up in normal conversation?"

He rolls his eyes but I can tell he's embarrassed and trying to play it off. "My parents asked about the students I tutor, and I told them one did really good on her test. My sister overheard, and well..." He gestures to the sticker on the back of my hand. "That's from her."

I hold out my hand and let the sticker sparkle under the library lights. "Tell her thank you. I love it."

"You earned it," he says with a laugh. "Now let's get to business."

As much as I want to argue and try to blow off studying, I don't. Jonah has proven to be a great tutor so far and I'm actually getting excited about seeing all my grades go up. We do my homework and study for my upcoming math test. With fifteen minutes left of tutoring, I start in on some extra credit worksheets. I finish the second one when I remember what these things mean.

"Can I still ask a question?" I ask, placing the completed worksheet on top of his notebook. "One question per worksheet?"

"What more could you possibly want to know about me?" Jonah asks, tilting his head while he looks over my paper.

I shrug. "You're still a mystery, Jonah."

He rolls his eyes. "I'm going to take that as a yes," I say, sitting straighter. "Have you ever kissed a girl on a date and then gone four days without texting her?"

"That's oddly specific," he says, furrowing his brow.

"Answer the question."

He finishes scanning my answers on the worksheet and puts it at the bottom of the stack. "No. I only kiss girls I'm dating, and if I'm dating a girl then I don't go that long without talking to her."

I rest my chin in my hand while I watch him. "So…if you ask a girl on a date but then you bring your friends with you to the date, is it still considered a date?"

"One question per worksheet," he says.

I shove the second paper at him. "I did two already."

"Natalie…" he says with a sigh. "I agreed to answer questions about *myself*, not to give you covert dating advice."

"I am asking about you. Would *you* consider that a date?"

He contemplates it for a moment. "Maybe. But not really. A date is something intimate."

I open my mouth to say more, but he points at the stack of papers. "One question per paper."

I blow a raspberry at him and get back to work, flipping through the pages until I find one with only four questions. Jonah's phone buzzes and he texts back to whoever texted him. It takes a lot of willpower on my end not to ask who he's talking to, because I know he'll try to count that as my question for this worksheet.

When I'm finished, I hand it to him. "What did you mean the other day at lunch when you said you think you *hopefully* deserve better than Lara?"

He stares at the worksheet while he thinks about it. "It means I think I deserve better than the kind of girls I've dated lately," he says after a moment. I stare at him until he gives me more information. "I'm not an asshole, okay? I'm a good person. I'm nice. I don't cheat on girls or have random hookups that don't mean anything. I don't think it's too much to want a girl to be nice to me in return, you know?"

I nod, thinking that's all I'll get out of him, but now he's looking off in the distance, his thoughts clearly focusing on the topic at hand. "I just…I'm not some popular jock and I'm not the most jacked manly-man ever, but that doesn't mean I should settle for someone who treats me like crap. So I said I *hopefully* deserve better, because I think I do. I don't mean to sound arrogant, it's just—" He sighs.

"I know what you mean," I say, finding the words he can't seem to say. "You are a good guy. You *do* deserve better than your ex-girlfriend. There's nothing wrong in admitting that."

"You should take some of your own advice," he says, poking me in the arm with his pen.

I lift an eyebrow. "What do you mean?"

"A guy kissed you then didn't text you for four days?" He shakes his head. "Ditch that asshole. He's not worth it."

"That was a hypothetical," I say quickly. "Totally not real."

His lips flatten as he looks at me and I know he's not buying it.

The librarian clears her throat and I realize she's looking at us. "Tutoring and detention are over," she says with an exhausted wave of her hand. "Time to get out of here. You're the last ones left."

"Crap," I say, looking down at our table filled with papers and books. We totally talked past the bell that dismissed us from tutoring. Jonah and I gather up our stuff. The last thing he grabs is his notebook, which is opened to my page.

"Hey," he says, tilting it toward me. "Today marks our one month of tutoring completed." He grins in this boyish way, like he's truly proud of the accomplishment. "Only one month left."

"That's definitely cooler than talking about my dating failures," I say as I sling my backpack over my shoulder.

"I thought you were speaking in hypotheticals," he says as he walks toward the parking lot.

I smirk. "Shut up."

As we reach the glass doors that lead into the parking lot, it's clear today's weather has taken a turn from sunny and pretty to ugly and gross.

"Ugh," I say as we watch the dark clouds light up with a streak of lightning. Thunder cracks and the leaves on nearby trees blow. "There's no way I can walk home before it starts raining." I pull out my phone and unlock the screen. "Hopefully there's no customers at the store so Mom can come get me real fast."

"I'll drive you home," Jonah says. His car keys are already in his hand and he gives them a shake. "My car is totally rainproof inside."

I roll my eyes. "You're a dork."

"A dork with a car." He pushes open the door and holds it for me to walk outside. "Come on, I'll drive you."

"I can't bum a ride off you," I say as I reluctantly step outside into the cool windy air. "I'll just jog home and maybe I'll beat the rain."

"Absolutely not." Jonah hooks his arm through mine and tugs me along. "I'm happy to give you a ride. Actually..." he turns to me, looking down a little since he's taller than I am. I'm so close to him I can smell his soapy skin and see the flecks of gold in his brown eyes. Since our arms are halfway linked, my hand reaches up on its own and grabs his bicep. He flexes it just a little when I touch him, either on purpose or on reflex.

"Actually what?" I say, realizing he never finished his sentence.

"I think we should go get frozen yogurt, if you're up for it. It can be a celebration of being halfway through tutoring."

I can't think of anything better than spending more time with Jonah right now. Mom needs me at the store, but she can wait another half an hour. It's not like we're ever busy on Tuesdays.

"Okay," I say with a grin. "Sounds fun."

Jonah's car smells like leather and Armor All. He's a good driver who doesn't take the turns too fast like Caleb did. He talks about school to pass the time, but I wish we'd get back to more important topics, like what kind of girl he wants to date.

We fill our own cups of yogurt and add toppings. I choose cherry yogurt with dark chocolate chips and coconut shreds. Jonah gets the birthday cake flavor, saying it's so good it doesn't need any toppings, but then he covers it with sprinkles, brownie bites, and whipped cream anyway. When we get to the register, I set mine down and reach for my wallet.

"I'm buying," Jonah says, handing over some money to the cashier, a tall girl who looks like she's fed up with working here.

"What? No," I say. "I'll buy my own."

He shoves my hand away. "We're celebrating," he says, standing straighter which makes him seem much taller. "Let me celebrate you. Please?"

"Aww," the cashier says as her grumpy expression breaks into a smile. "That is *so* sweet."

"Okay," I say, relenting and putting my wallet back in my backpack. "Thank you."

He grins and holds out my yogurt for me. "You're welcome."

We make our way to a table in the corner of the room, right next to the window that shows the darkened sky that still hasn't opened up with rain yet. I watch Jonah as he moves his spoon around, flattening the whipped cream and then stabbing it. Now that I know Jonah for the person he is, he's not some brainy nerd like I first assumed when I met him. He's cute, and sweet, and he celebrates little things like halfway points in tutoring. It makes my heart beat in this crooked way, and suddenly I'm wishing I was the kind of girl that's good enough to date a guy like Jonah.

"I'm glad we're friends," I say, looking up at him. *Please say something*, I think. *Don't just let me get away with calling us friends. Say you want to be more.*

His smile reveals his shiny white teeth, and that little crinkle in his eyes. "I'm glad we're friends too."

19

I SEE MOM GLARING AT ME THROUGH THE WINDOW AS I APPROACH the Magpie. At first, I think it's just a trick of the light, and her face looks angrier than it really is, but once I rush inside, leaving the pouring rain behind me, I can tell for sure she's pissed. I just don't know why.

She's standing behind the front counter, her hair pulled into a messy bun with strands hanging down her face. Thin lines crease her forehead and her eyes are narrowed and looking right at me.

"Hey," I say, acting like I can't see the annoyance in her expression. I set my backpack down behind the front counter and look at the store. "Wow, there's actually shoppers here."

"A dozen of them," Mom says. "Why are you late? You're never late."

"Oh...I had tutoring—"

Mom rolls her eyes to the ceiling. "I know about the tutoring. I've been filling in for you for a month now. Today you're forty-five minutes later than usual and we've been *busy*." She gestures toward the door where the sky is darker than ever and the rain is really pouring now. I managed to get from Jonah's car to the store without getting too wet by sticking to the over-hanging eaves that line the boardwalk stores.

"I'm sorry," I say as I straighten a stack of business cards on the counter just for something to do. "I didn't realize we'd be busy."

"We've been much busier lately, especially with the new book selection, and it's very hard to run this place by myself, Natalie."

Her nostrils flare and I know she could go on griping at me, but a woman comes up to ask her a question about the hand-made glass vases. I take the opportunity to leave the counter and I wander around the store saying hello to customers and straightening up the merchandise. As much as I'd loved having frozen yogurt with Jonah, now I'm regretting it a little bit. I had no idea we'd be this busy, but people tend to stay in stores longer when it's raining outside. I should have thought of that.

Still. Mom should be *happy*, not pissed. We have customers! We're making money. This is a good thing. And so what; even if she is mad at me, more customers mean Jack Brown can't talk us into selling the store.

After we close the Magpie for the night, Mom seems to have gotten over her anger at me. We earned four hundred dollars today, which is a huge sales day for a Tuesday, which is usually one of our worst days. Mom seems happy about it as she counts the money from the register.

I want to tell her about my grades getting better, but I'm afraid that'll make her think of tutoring again and then she'll go back to being annoyed with me.

At home, I head up to my room and that's when all of the stuff in my real life comes back to me. At work, it's easier to shove aside thoughts of guys and dates because I have to focus on the store. But now, at nine o'clock on a school night, when my hair is wet from my shower, and there's nothing to do but lie awake in bed, I start thinking about it all again.

Jonah made it pretty clear that we're friends. That's a good thing, I guess. I don't need some stupid teenage love triangle between Caleb and Jonah—I just need to focus on one guy I like. I stare at my phone and pull up my text messages. Besides April, the last text I have is from Jonah. It was all the smiley faces he sent me for my test grade. Below that are texts from my mom, my aunt Sheryl, and Jessica from my chemistry class who wanted to know the password to ChemXLabs.

And even further down the list is Caleb's name. *ha ha. Be there to pick you up in five mins*

I click on the message and send him a new one. He kissed me, and I want to get to the bottom of this. Does he like me or not?

Me: I'm sick of this rainy weather!

I turn on my television and flip through the channels as I wait for a reply. After twenty minutes, my phone beeps.

Caleb: me too. freaking sucked setting up for OL today.

It takes me minute to know what he's talking about, but then I remember that Operation Lunch is tomorrow. Every year, the student council throws an outdoor lunch on campus to raise funds for whatever charity they've chosen this time. Local businesses donate pizzas and burgers and stuff that the school sells for charity, and we all eat outside and play games. I guess he had to set up the game booths today in the rain.

Me: That sucks

Caleb: tell me about it. I don't know why they make the football team do it every year. We have a perfectly capable baseball, basketball, and soccer team. Smh

Me: haha…at least it's for charity? You could put it on your college applications

Caleb: no need to suck up on applications. They all want me for football

I don't know what to say back, so I decide to be the mysterious girl again and I leave him hanging. He doesn't write back though, and I wonder if he finds me mysterious or just boring.

AT LUNCH THE NEXT DAY, APRIL AND I MEET UP AT HER LOCKER. Everyone is excited for Operation Lunch because a local pizza shop donated fifty macaroni and cheese pizzas in addition to the normal ones. April wants to try it out, so we get in the long line in front of the pizza food truck.

Luckily, yesterday's bad weather went away last night and today is bright and sunny again with a cool breeze brought in from the storm.

"So I texted him last night," I say, keeping my voice low so no one in line can overhear me.

"Which him?" April asks.

I give her a look. "There's only one guy in my life."

She tilts her head. "Technically there's two, but you're too scared to admit it."

I'm not a violent person, but I get the sudden urge to stomp on her foot to make her shut up. Instead, I say, "I texted *Caleb*. He didn't really seem too interested in talking to me."

"He's a dude," she says with a shrug. "You have to lay it on thick to get a message across to them." She folds her arms across her chest and looks out at the courtyard. I follow her gaze.

There he is. Caleb and his football friends are tossing around a football. The picnic benches that line the courtyard are filled with cheerleaders and other popular girls, who are picking at their food and watching the boys show off. Caleb's right in the middle, wearing jeans and a white T-shirt. He intercepts a football pass and holds the ball in the air, doing a victory pump.

I can't believe he kissed me. A guy as popular as that, with gorgeous eyes and the perfect athlete's build. I must look like I'm swooning pretty hard because April smacks me in the arm.

"Move," she says, gesturing to the food line which has moved forward about five steps since I've been zoning out. I catch up with her and glance back at the courtyard.

"Your dating life is so fascinating to me," April says.

"Shut up," I tell her. I can't seem to stop looking at Caleb, who is now leaning over and allowing one of the cheerleaders feed him pizza.

I roll my eyes and turn back to face April.

"Ouch," she says, glancing at Caleb. "Are you sure you like him?"

"He made the first move on me," I say defensively. "He asked me out. It's not my fault I like him…it's not like I'm hopelessly crushing on him… I mean there has to be a chance, right? He kissed me." I say the last part as quietly as possible.

She shrugs. "I just think the two guys in your life are such total opposites that it's kind of hilarious. I wouldn't pick Caleb, if I were you. I'd pick him."

She turns her gaze toward the parking lot, where a section of it has been roped off for the game booths and food vendors. The band has set up their annual face painting booth, which is something they have to fight for because every year the administration tries to shut them down since going back to class with painted faces is kind of a huge distraction.

Jonah's not in the band, but he must have volunteered anyway because he's wearing a white smock from the art room to protect his clothes while he sits on a stool with a pallet of paint balanced in his left hand.

Mrs. Mindy, the elementary special education teacher, is standing next to him with a few younger kids in tow. They must have walked over from the elementary across the street. A little girl with a disability is sitting in a folding chair next to him, clutching a baby doll in her hands. She looks scared, and Mrs. Mindy is talking to her.

Jonah says something that makes her smile. She points to the board of face paint designs, choosing a pink heart. When Jonah leans forward to paint her cheek, she shakes her head and starts crying.

Mrs. Mindy kneels down beside her, but the girl's focus is on Jonah. I can't hear what he says, but whatever it is, it makes the girl smile. She pushes out her baby doll toward him and he paints a pink heart on the doll's cheek.

The girl is all smiles now. After contemplating it for a few seconds, she turns her cheek to Jonah. Mrs. Mindy beams as Jonah paints the heart on the girl's cheek to match the one on her doll.

"Oh…my…God…." April breathes. She clutches my arm while we both watch the scene unfold. "Is that not the most adorable thing ever? He's good with kids," she says, tugging me forward as we move up in line. She puts a hand to her chest. "I want a guy like that."

My heart aches in my chest, and if life were perfect, of course I'd choose Jonah. I shove down the pain I feel as I tear my eyes away from him and focus on the food truck instead. "He's all yours," I say, trying to act like I don't care.

"No he's not," April says. "I would never take a guy from you. I'm just saying, I want someone *like* him."

I shrug and look back at Caleb, trying to find something redeeming in the way he's gloating around the courtyard like he's the king of football. "Jonah just wants to be friends, April. I can't keep thinking about him or talking about him, okay? It's too painful. I need to focus on guys who do like me."

She looks like she wants to object but I press my lips together. "I'm serious. Let's not talk about him anymore."

We get our pizza and choose a shady spot under some oak trees to eat lunch. We don't say much, and I know we're still thinking about the Jonah thing. It was insanely adorable how well he made that little girl laugh and forget about her fears. It tugs at my heartstrings. But I've made a rule not to talk about Jonah, and I'm going to stick with it.

"Umm," April says when lunch is almost over.

"What?" I say, but it's too late. Whoever she's looking at behind me has just walked up and sat next to us.

Jonah takes a long sip from his can of Cherry Coke. "Hey. Can you believe they actually held this thing on April 1st?" he says, glancing at April who looks like her eyes are about to burst out of her head. Luckily, he has no idea that we were just talking about him.

"What do you mean?" I ask.

"April Fools' Day." He shrugs. "They scheduled Operation Lunch on a joke day, so I was afraid people wouldn't take it seriously. Luckily, they did."

"Wow, it's April already?" I glance at April, who nods.

"It's the best month of the year!" she says in this goofy way. "When I was a kid, I called it *me* month."

"I guess I wasn't paying attention," I say, realizing my birthday is only two days away. I'll be eighteen and a legal adult. Too bad I don't feel like one. "This year is going by fast."

There's an awkwardness in the air that I'm positive Jonah picks up on. "Sorry for barging in," he says, bending back on his knees. "I won't take long. I just wanted to ask about your work hours."

I lift an eyebrow. "At The Magpie?"

He nods. "You said you work after school every day?"

"Yep. Until six. Why?"

He takes another sip from his drink. "I just wanted to check out the books."

"You can buy a book anytime," April says with a hint of flirtation in her voice. "Why does Natalie need to be there?"

I could kill her for what she's implying, but Jonah just smiles and stands up. "You're right," he says with a chuckle. "See you at tutoring, Nat."

We watch him walk away just far enough to be out of earshot and then I glare at April. She holds up her hands defensively. "Sorry, *Nat*. The boy wants to see you after school," she says, wiggling her eyebrows. "Plus he called you Nat. Casual friends don't give each other nicknames."

"I said we aren't talking about him anymore." There's a lump in my throat and it feels hard to breathe, but I think that's just my heart's way of telling me I totally screwed up. I should have been nice to Jonah from the start. Maybe he would have liked me in the way I like him.

"I don't think you're over him," April says softly. "I'm just calling it like I see it."

Caleb and his friends jog past us, chasing after a ball that got kicked way too far.

"Let me prove it to you," I say as I gather up my courage. I cup my hands to my mouth and yell, "Hey, Caleb!"

He looks around, and then nods when he sees me wave at him. "Sup, Natalie?"

I'm aware that a few people are still out here, some of them looking in my direction. I don't care. I have to prove to myself that I'm over Jonah once and for all. "You wanna go out me with on Wednesday?"

Beside me, April gasps. My heart beats so fast it might explode, and I watch Caleb's eyebrows shoot up at my unexpected invitation.

"Yeah," he calls back as someone tosses him the ball. "Sounds fun."

20

CALEB TOSSES THE FOOTBALL BACK TO SOME GUY AND THEN I have his full attention. As much as I've wanted just that, having Caleb's eyes on me is kind of intimidating. I wonder how many people are watching this exchange right now. April has slipped off somewhere, probably to give me time alone with him, but I kind of wish she was here right now.

"So what'd you have in mind?" Caleb asks, giving me a grin just like he had when we'd kissed at the arcade.

"Wednesday," I say as we walk. I'm not sure what I want to do, and I probably should have figured it out before I yelled his name and asked him on a date.

"This Wednesday?" he asks, lifting an eyebrow.

"Yep. The third. Should we go to the beach and hang out at that bonfire that's always lit?"

He nods. "Yeah, I could do that. But why Wednesday? Why not the weekend so we can stay out late?"

"It'll be April 3rd, which is my birthday," I say with a grin. My answer makes him stiffen.

"Your birthday? Am I supposed to get you a gift?" He laughs

and holds open the door to the school for me. "I wouldn't even know what to get."

"No, not at all," I say quickly, hoping he doesn't think I asked him out just to get free stuff. "I just wanted to have a chill night. Maybe we can get a cupcake from Gigi's on the boardwalk then hang out by the bonfire?"

"Uh, sure," he says after thinking about it for a few seconds. Down the hallway, some guy calls his name. He nods at him, holding up a finger to signal that he'll be right there. "Just text me or something."

And then he jogs to catch up with his friend, leaving me in the crowded hallway after lunch, reeling over my newly found confidence. I asked a guy out. And he said yes.

The next two days fly by, and the next thing I know it's Wednesday, April 3rd. My birthday. Mom's still asleep when I leave the house in the morning, so I don't bother waking her up. When I was a little kid, she'd make me smiley face pancakes and let me open one present before school. Now that I'm older, birthdays really aren't a big deal. Sometimes I miss being a kid.

April is waiting for me on the sidewalk when I leave my house. Usually we meet in the middle of our houses, but today she's holding a gift bag piled high with tissue paper.

"Happy birthday!" she says, rushing up the steps to my porch. "I thought I'd meet you here so you can leave your gift at home and not have to lug it around all day."

I grin as she hands me the bag. "Thank you," I say before I even open it. I didn't realize how bummed out I felt about Mom sleeping in until now. It's not every day that your daughter turns eighteen.

April has given me a new Circle E Candle in my absolute favorite scent, Barefoot Beach. It's the big one too, the one that costs more and is harder to find in stores. I clutch it to my chest. "You are an angel," I say as I close my eyes and hug the candle. "Thank you so much."

She grins and gives me a hug. "You're totally welcome. Mom and I found it like three months ago when we went to Dallas, and I've been saving it for you."

I head back inside to drop off my gift and Mom's still not awake. Oh well, I tell myself. I'm an adult now. I don't need my mom to wish me a happy birthday.

"So have you talked to Caleb yet?" April asks on our walk to school. Although we haven't texted at all since Operation Lunch, Caleb has said "Hi" to me in the hallways yesterday and the day before.

April has been telling me to chat him up through text, but I never do. I contacted him first last time, and I'm waiting for him to contact me this time. I shake my head.

"He knows it's your birthday today, so he better freaking text you," she says. "If not, I'm going to kick his ass."

I roll my eyes. "He's a guy…guys are dumb, remember?"

"So why do we like them again?" she asks.

I heave a sigh. Sometimes I really don't know the answer to that.

My school day is easy enough. Tutoring went really well yesterday and Jonah and I finally got caught up with the lessons my teachers are giving in class, so I breeze by today with no problems. I take notes and I focus and I mark places in the book that I don't quite understand so Jonah can help me with them at our next tutoring session. I'm starting to breathe easier when it comes to school now. I haven't missed any more days, so everything is going according to the plan Mrs. Reese set up for me. I might actually graduate now.

April and I eat lunch together, and I resist the urge to look over at Caleb's table. I don't know what I was hoping for—a Happy Birthday? A hello? —but it's like Caleb doesn't realize I have the same lunch as him.

It's not until sixth period when he finally acknowledges my existence.

"There's the birthday girl," Caleb says as he walks up next to me in the art hallway. I can smell his cologne before I smell him, and I wonder how long we'll need to date before I can politely tell him to lay off the stuff. One spritz is all anyone needs.

"I am officially eighteen now," I say.

"You should go by a lottery ticket," he says, his grin making me swoon. "And anything else you can do as an eighteen-year-old. Like check out a porn shop or something."

"Ew," I say. "Aren't there just perverts in porn shops?"

He shrugs. "And people who just turned eighteen who are using all their new age privilege."

I laugh. "So what time do you want to hang out tonight?"

"I don't know," he says. "Just text me?"

I nod. "I'll talk to you later."

"Later," he says. Then he leans over and touches my lower back, his hand sliding down until it covers my back pocket. "Happy Birthday."

I blush from head to toe and I watch him until he walks into his classroom.

MY AUNT SHERYL AND A FEW OF MY COUSINS TEXT ME HAPPY Birthday. But by the time I get to the store after school, I'm pretty sure my mom has forgotten that today her only child turns eighteen. She's wearing her reading glasses and she's bent over the inventory list, highlighting items as she goes along.

"Hey," I say, dropping my backpack behind the front counter. "Busy day?"

She snorts. "Hardly. Not a single customer since lunch."

I watch her for a moment, wondering if she'll suddenly remember. I don't expect a present or anything, since money is so tight right now. But I do want some kind of acknowledgement. She doesn't say anything at all though, she just crunches her brows together and stares at the paperwork as if it's the inventory's problem that no customers come into the store.

Mom has a lot on her mind, and that's what I tell myself as the next hour goes by and she still hasn't realized it's my birthday. I straighten some items on the shelves and look up more books to order for the store. It's only four-thirty, but Caleb hasn't yet replied to the text I sent him an hour ago.

Me: Gigi's cupcakes at 5?

I stare at the text, wondering if I should say something else. At 4:45, I send another one.

Me: Headed to Gigi's! Meet me there!

"Hey, Mom?" I ask. She makes some kind of noise, but doesn't look up from the books.

"Since the store isn't busy, can I head out for an hour or so? I'm meeting a friend for cupcakes."

The word *cupcakes* should trigger her into remembering it's my birthday. But she just nods and says, "Sure. I'll call you if we miraculously get busy, but I'm betting that won't happen."

So yeah, my feelings are a little hurt that my own mother forgot my birthday, but I'm starting to worry about her. She's so preoccupied with the store and so stressed out all the time about money. Once stress makes you forget birthdays, something should be done. I need to find a way to save The Magpie once and for all, so Mom can rest. She could take a vacation and enjoy life again without worrying about paying the bills.

I walk down to Gigi's Cupcakes and order the birthday cake flavored cupcake. I get a coffee as well, and I sit in a corner booth and eat them because by 5:30, I'm starting to think Caleb isn't going to show. I debate texting him again.

I finish my cupcake and wander down the boardwalk to the bonfire on the beach, but none of the benches have Caleb sitting there waiting on me. I go back to Gigi's an hour later and order another cupcake, this time the double chocolate one with a mound of icing on top that's taller than the cake itself.

I eat the whole thing.

Still no text from Caleb.

Happy Birthday to me. Ugh.

Mom has probably closed up the shop by now, but I walk back there to get my backpack. The lights are still on, the OPEN sign still facing outward, even though it's fifteen minutes past closing. I guess Mom forgot about closing time just like she forgot my birthday.

I come to a stop on the boardwalk just a few feet before the entrance to the Magpie. I stare up at the setting sun, look around at the stores, half of them now owned by Jack Brown Properties.

Jack Brown is trying to ruin my mother's business, and his son just ruined my birthday. I check my phone again, just in case, but there are no new messages. Tears well up in my eyes. I blink and they roll down my cheeks. I shouldn't feel sorry for myself, but here I am, doing just that.

Some birthday.

Congratulations, Natalie. You picked a total asshole to ask out on a date.

21

I don't want Mom to see me like this, so I dry my eyes. I think about walking home, but I'm not really in the mood to spend a forty-five-minute walk thinking about how Caleb stood me up and totally ruined my birthday.

With a deep breath, I push open the door to The Magpie and turn the OPEN sign to CLOSED.

"Natalie!" Mom says from the front desk. She rushes around it and sweeps me into a hug. "I'm so sorry, baby! I can't believe I forgot your birthday!"

She squeezes me so hard all the air leaves my lungs and I struggle to draw in another breath. "It's okay," I mumble.

"No, it's not! I'm so mad at myself." Mom pulls back, holding me at arms' length while she looks me over. "You're so grown up and mature now, sweetheart. Let's close up and go get dinner, okay? I'll make it up to you."

I shake my head. "Mom, we can't afford restaurant food right now."

"Not another word, Nat! We can afford it for your birthday. It's a special night."

"Seriously, Mom. I just had two of Gigi's cupcakes so I'm just really not into it."

Mom puts a hand to her chest and frowns at me. "But I feel so horrible, sweetheart! It's my daughter's birthday and I've been so absorbed in work, I completely forgot."

I shrug. "You remembered eventually. That's all that matters."

Mom frowns. "Actually… I didn't. Not at first." Guilt lines form in her forehead and I give her a weird look.

"But…you did remember. It's still my birthday."

She shakes her head. "Your friend came by to see you and he made me realize what day it is."

My heart lifts. "Caleb?" So maybe he didn't ditch me tonight after all. Maybe his phone broke or he lost my number or something. I glance out at the boardwalk. He could be out there waiting for me right now.

"Caleb?" Mom says, her voice high-pitched. "You have two boyfriends now?"

My cheeks flush. "I don't have any boyfriends, Mom."

Mom walks to the counter and leans down behind it. When she stands back up, she's holding a purple vase of sunflowers and red roses. My jaw drops.

"This boy's name was Jonah," she says, giving me a look like I should be ashamed of myself for not knowing which boy came to see me.

It feels like my legs are numb as I walk toward the counter, where a beautiful display of flowers is waiting for me.

"He also got you this," Mom says, setting down a small cake box. I open the lid and find a personal sized chocolate cake. White icing letters on top say *Happy Birthday Nat*. My stomach twists in a painful way. Jonah did all of this for me?

I pull out the card attached to the flowers.

Have a wonderful 18th!
Your favorite study geek,

Jonah

My lip quivers and I bite down on it. "Mom, do you mind if I...?"

"Yes," she says with a laugh. "Go find the boy. He seemed so disappointed that you weren't here when he stopped by." Mom winks at me. "He was cute."

I flush a deep red and grab my phone from my back pocket, rushing outside the store to call him so my mom won't overhear.

He picks up on the second ring, and I can hear the smile in his voice.

"Hello, birthday girl."

"Thank you for the flowers," I say, feeling like a simple thank you isn't enough. "And the cake. It's adorable."

"You're welcome," he says. "The cake is from Mary's Bakery off sixth street. My family gets one for me every year on my birthday. They're really good."

I bite my lip. "How did you know it was my birthday?"

"Your ChemXLabs password. Zero four, zero three."

I laugh. "I can't believe you remembered that."

"We've only logged in to ChemXLabs like a hundred times," he says with a laugh. "I'm sorry I missed you today. You said you worked all the time, so I thought you'd be there."

I should have been there. I shouldn't have been out waiting on a guy who would just stand me up. I should have been at the store where I said I'd be. Then I could have seen Jonah.

"I'm sorry," I say with a sigh. "I'm normally there. Today was just...an off day."

There's a silence for a few seconds and I start talking because I'm not ready to get off the phone. "So all that talk about wanting to buy a book was just a ruse, huh?"

"Yes," he says. "I mean...I wanted to look at the books too, but your mom was there and I talked to her and I just felt awkward so I left."

"Oh no… What did my mom say? Please tell me it wasn't embarrassing?"

He laughs. "Oh, it was so embarrassing. She told me every humiliating story about you that she could think of."

"What!"

He laughs. "I'm just playing. She was really nice. I was just nervous. It's super awkward bringing flowers for someone's daughter. And then she freaked, because apparently, she forgot your birthday."

"Yeah…only you and April remembered," I say. Technically Caleb remembered today, but he also blew me off so I won't count that. "The flowers are so beautiful. Thank you so much, Jonah. I'm so lucky you're my friend. You've saved my birthday."

There's another long silence, and then some idiot on the beach screams out like he's howling at the moon. His buddies laugh, and the weird thing is that I can hear the same thing through Jonah's phone.

"Wait…where are you?" I ask.

"I'm on the beach. My mom's having her book club tonight and it's like six middle-aged ladies who drink wine and try to embarrass me every time they see me. I make an effort to stay away on book club nights."

"Where on the beach?" I say. "Can I come see you?"

"Um, sure. I'm by the bonfire."

"Give me five minutes," I say, and then I hang up. I tell Mom I'll walk home tonight and she takes my cake and flowers home with her in the car. After we lock up, I comb my fingers through my hair and check my reflection in the glass window of the shop. There's not much I can do looks-wise right now, but I'm okay. I'd dressed up for Caleb, after all.

Speaking of Caleb, I check my phone again and nothing. I should be hurt, I guess, but I'm really just pissed. Pissed at Caleb for lying to me, and pissed at myself for going after a guy like him.

The setting sun casts an orange-red glow on the ocean, and it illuminates the golden sand beneath my feet. The bonfire is about ten feet wide and it's usually burning every night during the summer, thanks to the college frat boys who tend to it. I find Jonah sitting on a beach towel, wearing khaki shorts and a blue and white plaid button up shirt. The sleeves are rolled up to his elbows, and I'm really liking this look on him.

When he sees me, he smiles, and I smile too. "Hey."

"Hi," I say, feeling shy for the first time ever. He slides over so there's room on his oversized beach towel.

"Want to sit with me?"

I sit next to him and watch as the flames from the bonfire dance off his face. "Why are you out here by yourself?" I ask.

He shrugs and leans back on his hands. "Just thinking."

"About what?"

He shrugs again. I lean over and nudge him in the shoulder with my own. "I'll tell you what I've been thinking," I say. Sometimes, it still feels like it used to back when we first started tutoring and I could mess with him and not feel awkward. Right now is one of those times.

"What are you thinking?" he asks. It could be my imagination, but I think his eyes flit to my lips before looking back at the bonfire.

"I'm thinking that I wish I had done things differently when we first met."

"Like pay attention?" he says sarcastically. I shove him with my shoulder again.

"No."

"Like do your extra credit worksheets more often so you wouldn't have so many still left to do by now?"

I roll my eyes. "No, Jonah."

"Then what?" he says, his eyes meeting mine.

The fire dances off his face, and I know this is one of those moments that will require a huge amount of courage.

"Like get to know you," I say. "Like be your friend instead of think of you as the smart guy enemy."

"And what would that have done?" he asks, his voice lower.

I shrug. "Maybe things could have done differently. Maybe I wouldn't just be your friend." I say the last word like it annoys me.

"What's wrong with being friends?" he asks, each word he says slow and deliberate.

"Jonah…" I stare down at my hands as they smooth out the towel on the sand. "I think you know what I'm talking about. As soon as I realized I liked you, I'd already screwed everything up."

"Maybe," he says. "But it wasn't irreversible damage."

I look at him, and he's looking at me. He seems closer than before, his head tipped toward mine. I can smell his shampoo, see the flecks of gold in his eyes as he leans closer to me. "Maybe we can start over," he says softly.

He leans toward me, so close I can I can see his lip tremble as he draws in a breath. I'm moving too, tipping my mouth up to meet his as he brings his lips, slightly parted, to mine.

My heart pounds, and my lips warm as they press against his mouth, pausing for just a second before he deepens the kiss. My whole body warms and aches to touch him. I want to wrap my arms around his neck, tangle my hands in his hair, press my skin against his.

But a kiss is all he gives me. His hands stay rooted to the beach towel as if he's trying to control himself. When the kiss ends, his face stays close, his forehead pressing against mine. He exhales softly, his eyes closed. My lips tingle, desperately wanting to kiss him again.

"You said something about starting over?" I whisper.

Jonah smiles and it reaches all the way to his eyes. "Yeah," he says, reaching up and brushing my hair behind my ear. "We should start over."

I sit up and hold out my hand. "Hi, I'm Natalie. I think we go to school together."

He shakes my hand. "I'm Jonah. I think I'm your tutor."

I laugh and he doesn't let go of my hand, he just slides his fingers into mine and then pulls our intertwined hands against his chest. "Now that the introductions are over," he says, bringing my hand up to his lips. "Can we kiss again?"

I grin. "That sounds like a great way to get to know each other."

2 2

I BARELY SLEEP AT ALL. AFTER OUR MAKE OUT SESSION ON THE beach, Jonah drove me home and kissed me goodnight. Now, I lay awake in bed replaying those few minutes over and over in my head. He'd grinned at me, his face glowing from the dome light in his Lexus. I had my passenger door open, my foot on the ground, but I wasn't ready to leave the car yet.

"So," he'd said after kissing me softly on the lips. "Tomorrow we go back to school."

"Well, it is Thursday," I said. "So that sounds about right."

He grinned. "Will everything be different now?"

Now that we've kissed, he meant, even though he didn't say it. I nodded. "Yes."

"Is that a good thing?"

I could see the hesitation behind his eyes, the momentary panic that maybe our kissing excursion was a bad, bad idea. But after the few weeks I've had getting to know him, and realizing how stupid I'd been in liking some asshole like Caleb, I knew it wasn't a bad idea.

It was a perfect idea.

"It's a really good thing," I said.

And then, because Jonah is not at all like Caleb and the other guys who treat girls poorly, Jonah texted me goodnight.

I grab my phone from my nightstand and read it again.

Jonah: Goodnight :)

My heart floods with warm mushy feelings every time I read it. But now it's almost one in the morning, and I desperately need to sleep so I have enough energy to stay awake tomorrow morning. Somehow, I manage to fall asleep, and before I know it, my alarm is buzzing and it's Thursday morning, and it's time to face another day at school.

As I'm getting dressed—and spending a little too much time on my appearance for Jonah's sake—my phone beeps. I set down my flat iron.

April: Migraine… kill me… not going to school…

Me: Ugh, I'm sorry! Feel better!

I study myself in the mirror, feeling a little guilty at how relieved I am over April's text. Not about her migraine—I feel horrible about that. She has this condition where she gets one about once a month, and it's so bad she can't function. She just takes these prescription migraine pills that make her feel sick and only reduce about half of the pain and she lays in her room all day with the windows covered to block out the sun.

That part makes me feel really bad for her, because it's a terrible condition to have. But I'm also relieved because I didn't know how to act around her today. I mean…I kissed Jonah.

How do I tell my best friend she was right and I totally like him after all the times I said I didn't?

I'm totally not looking forward to hearing her jump around and sing the *I Told You So* song when she finds out. My phone beeps again.

Jonah: Good morning! Would you and April like a ride to school?

A boy who texts goodnight and good morning? What is this

strange feeling I have? Oh, right. It's called being treated with respect.

I'm grinning so hard my cheeks hurt as I type out a reply to his message.

Me: April is sick today, but I don't want you to go out of your way. I can walk. :)

Jonah: It's not out of my way. What time should I be there?

Me: Where do you live?

Jonah: Off 4th St....

Me: That's totally far away!!

Jonah: So?

I bite the inside of my lip in a futile attempt to stop smiling. This boy is so sweet. I tell him he can come get me but only for today because I don't want him going out of his way every day of the week. Plus, I'm not going to be the kind of friend who ditches her best friend when she starts dating a guy. I know April, and she wouldn't want to be the third wheel in Jonah's car every morning. Maybe just on the days when it rains. Besides that, we'll keep walking to school.

I feel like walking into school with Jonah by my side will be this big event, like people will turn and watch us and we'll be walking in slow motion down the hallways together with all eyes on us. Turns out we're totally not even slightly popular, and no one cares. We don't hold hands, but we walk closer than usual. I want to reach for his hand, but it's all so new to me. Being around Jonah at the beach felt different, like we were new people outside of school. But now that I'm here with him in the familiar hallways of Sterling High, he almost feels like my annoying tutor again.

"Nat?" Jonah says just after the warning bell rings. He's walked me to my first period class and we're standing outside the door. "I don't want to push anything you don't want. Like... we don't have to spend all day together or anything. I really like you." He brushes my arm with his fingers as if he wants to reach for my hand but it's too awkward and there's no time. I grin up at him, unable to make my face stay normal for very long. Just seeing his cute expression while he figures out what to say makes me want to smile.

"I really like you too," I say.

His cheeks redden. "If I do something you don't like...just tell me, okay? I can slow down or give you space, or whatever."

"Why are you so worried?" I ask, poking him in the stomach.

He shrugs. "I just want to do this right. I want to make you happy. Not rush into things..."

"I can practically see the list you've made in your head," I tell him. "Dating is not like tutoring, Jonah. You can't just write up a study plan and check off each step." I give him a reassuring smile. Somehow, seeing how nervous he is makes me more confident. "We're going to be fine."

JONAH AND I FIND EACH OTHER AT THE START OF LUNCH. I'D TOLD him I wouldn't have anyone to sit with today since April is gone and he happily offered to sit with me. I don't know how this is going to work with our separate lunch tables, or what will happen when April comes back, but I'm looking forward to having this day alone with him.

We take our food out to the courtyard, which is a little uglier now that the school fenced in the portion around the cafeteria doors. Too many kids were caught walking off campus during their lunch break and not returning. Now we're allowed to eat outside, but only in the designated fenced in parts.

Jonah and I choose a bench near the fence and I notice Natasha O'Hurn lift an eyebrow as we walk past her and her band friends. She doesn't stop looking at us, even when we sit down and start eating our lunch. She probably doesn't even realize I'm watching her watch us, because she's looking at Jonah with an obvious hint of jealousy in her gaze.

"So your mom's store is pretty cool," Jonah says. He grabs a Cheeto and crunches it. "I think my mom goes in there sometimes. It has all that girly stuff she likes."

"Well, tell her to go there more often," I say with a snort. "And tell her to bring about five hundred rich friends to buy stuff so we don't go out of business."

"Are sales still bad?" he asks.

I nod and take a bite of my PB&J. "Selling books is helping, but not really. The bottom line still says we're screwed."

Jonah seems concerned, like he actually cares, when he asks some more questions. I get the feeling that talking sales and numbers appeals to his nerdy side, and that he's not just asking me stuff to be polite, so I tell him all about the store. About how my mom married my ex stepdad and the store was their dream. I even tell him about Mrs. Reese the AP, and how she showed me my paper from freshman year when I wanted to open a coffee shop next door. Jonah thinks a coffee shop is a great idea since oddly, there aren't any on the boardwalk already. Gigi's Cupcakes sells coffee, but not many people know that, plus her store is so small it doesn't have that *sit around and enjoy your coffee* vibe. My coffee shop would have that vibe.

By the time the bell rings, it only feels like we've been talking for a few minutes, not forty. I've never wanted to skip class more than I do now, so I could just stay out here with Jonah and talk all day. But now more than ever, I need to go to class. I want passing grades so that I can graduate, and so Jonah's perfect tutoring record can remain intact.

We pick up our trash and start heading toward the cafeteria door. Natasha and her friend are still watching us, her eyes narrowed in jealousy. I can't help but grin as I lace my arm through Jonah's and lay my head on his shoulder as we walk.

A couple of months ago, I wouldn't have cared one bit who

Jonah Garza was dating. He was a nerd, who hung with nerds, and I didn't want anything to do with that.

Now I see the error in my thinking. Jonah is so much more than a super-smart band-geek friend who never cuts class or gets into trouble.

He's kind, and hot, and a great kisser. He's patient, and clever, and he puts up with my crap. I feel like the luckiest girl in Sterling High.

My phone buzzes just after Jonah drops me off at my history class. My heart jumps with excitement as I slide out my phone and secretly check the screen under my desk. If it's Jonah telling me he misses me already, I might melt into goo from all the sweetness.

My heart gets stuck in my throat as I look at the text. It's not from Jonah.

Caleb: Hey boo, sry I was busy last nite. Wanna go out Friday?

23

THIS DAY IS GOING TOO WELL TO LET CALEB SCREW IT UP. I ignore his text. I even toss my phone in my backpack for the rest of the school day so I'm not tempted to check it. When the final bell rings, I sneak a look at it on my way to the library for tutoring. Caleb sent one more text, which was just a question mark. I smirk, satisfied that he's waiting around on me for once, and turn the phone off.

Even though we are technically dating now, Jonah is in full tutoring mode when I enter the library. He already has my chemistry notes open with the history textbook stacked underneath that.

"What kind of grades do you have?" I ask curiously as I take my seat next to him. "I'm guessing you make all A's."

"I have a one hundred average," he says, glancing down at the chemistry notes. "Want to study vocab first?"

"A one hundred in what?" I ask. "Which class?"

"All of them." I would think he's joking, but he looks right at me with all the seriousness he usually has.

"Wow," I say, exhaling. "Now I'm even more intimidated by you."

He snorts and shakes his head. "Nah, chica. Nothing to worry about. I'm the one intimidated by you."

I forget all about Caleb's stupid text while I study with Jonah. It feels a little weird to be so completely over the guy, since I crushed on him forever, but there's something about ditching a girl on her birthday that makes you severely unattractive. Plus, the more time I spend with Jonah, the more I realize how great it is to be with a guy who actually cares about you.

Jonah insists on driving me home after tutoring, but I tell him he can only do this on tutoring days because I can't leave April to walk home alone. He offers to bring her, but I tell him that's a little too fast. April needs to warm up to someone first. Plus, I like my walks home with her. It's our time to chat, relax, and enjoy the outside air. I wonder how much my life will change now that Jonah and I are a thing.

Since April's not here, and since I'm already getting a ride, I have Jonah drop me off at The Magpie so I don't have to ride my bike there. He kisses me in the parking lot, then grins at me as I reluctantly step out of his car. If it were up to me, we'd hang out all day, but I know the best way to have a good relationship is to give it some space. I can't make him tired of me this soon.

Mom is engrossed in a book when I walk in the store. She's sitting in one of the arm chairs in the break room, the hardback book just inches from her face.

"Hellooo," I say in a singsong as I tap on the doorframe.

She jumps. "When did you get here?"

I laugh. "Just now. Are you reading the merchandise?"

"No," she says, slamming the book closed. "Why? Is that unethical? If I read it but don't bend the pages and I never take it out of the store, is it still brand new?"

"You're going to have to figure that out on your own," I say, laughing as I go to the front desk and let her keep taking a break. I also take out my phone for the first time since lunch, because although I forget about Caleb when Jonah is around, now that he's gone, I'm wondering if Caleb has sent anything else.

And boy has he.

Caleb: ????

Caleb: Did you get my text?

Caleb: Hello?

Caleb: this Friday… me and you.

Caleb: we'll stay out late and I'll show you a good time

Caleb: I'll take your silence as a yes

My lip curls as I read his messages. What a disgusting pig.

Me: No need to blow up my phone. I had it turned off.

Caleb: there she is! You better wear something sexy on Friday

Funny how he can reply quickly today but was M.I.A. on my birthday.

Me: No thanks. I have plans on Friday

Caleb: Saturday then

Me: how about never? Does that work for you?

Caleb: never does not work. What's your problem? Lets go out!

Me: I said no. deal with it

Caleb: wow, girl. I like it when you play rough

I grip my phone and take a deep breath, telling myself not to give into my rage and throw it across the room. I can't afford a new phone and Caleb isn't worth it. I hate how cocky he is, how he thinks can just snap his fingers and I'll be thrilled to go out with him.

A few minutes go by and then he calls me. I ignore the call. When a customer comes in, it takes everything I have to put on a polite smile and be friendly even though all I want to do is go outside and take a deep breath and scream.

I'm checking out the customer's purchase—two metal bookmarks with charms on them—when the door opens again and

Caleb's stupid face grins at me. He doesn't seem affected at all that I basically told him to screw off in my last text.

Anger boils up inside me and for the first time ever, I wish I didn't work in The Magpie, so that he wouldn't be able to find me.

"Hey," he says in this pathetic seductive voice while he leans over the front counter. His body spray wafts through the room, assaulting my poor nose.

"Are you here to buy something?"

He glances around the store then looks back at me. "I'm here to talk to you."

I fold my arms over my chest, grateful that Mom is still in the back room and therefore out of earshot. "I have nothing to say to you."

"Why are you being so mean?" he says, crunching his eyebrows together as if he's really offended. Ha.

"You know what's mean?" I say, keeping my voice steady. "Standing up a girl on her birthday."

"Huh?" he says, before quickly bursting into a smile. "Oh that's nothing, Natalie. Wednesdays are stupid! We need to hang out this weekend so we can spend some quality time together."

"I'd rather eat my own socks."

He chuckles. "Look. Okay. You're mad." He rolls his eyes as if the idea of me being mad is just so unbelievably stupid. Maybe it is. Maybe if Jonah hadn't been there on the beach when I was having a horrible day…maybe I'd still be the pathetic girl who does whatever it takes for some attention from a cute boy.

"Let's talk, Natalie. I swear I'll make it up to you."

He gives me this sad little puppy face and it just makes me want to punch him. Mom appears from the back room, smiling when she sees I'm not alone.

"Hi there," she says. "Welcome to The Magpie."

"Thanks," Caleb tells her. "Me and Natalie were just talking."

"No, we weren't," I say.

Mom lifts an eyebrow, but I'm not about to bring her into my drama. "I was just telling him I'm busy at work."

"Give me a couple of minutes and I'll take over," Mom says, flashing me a smile as if she's doing me a favor. "Then you can go talk outside. Maybe get some ice cream?"

"Perfect!" Caleb says. He grins at me as if he's forgotten that I'm mad at him. "I'll see you outside." Then he bounces off with a pep in his step and I just want to punch something. How can he be such an ass?

But now I have to talk to him. I know without a doubt that he'll just come back in here and embarrass me in front of Mom if I don't. So when she's ready to take over for me, I slip outside, balling my fists at my sides.

I can't tell who's yelling at first. As I walk the boardwalk toward the ice cream shop, I hear low voices talking in angry tones coming from somewhere up ahead. Then I see the door to the game store, well, what used to be the game store, is open and the yelling is coming from outside.

I hear the name Caleb and stop. The angriest voice is Jack Brown's.

"I don't know," Caleb is saying. "She's pissed at me."

I lean closer, standing just outside the game store near the open door. Jack Brown says, "You were supposed to be charming, son. How did she get mad at you?"

"I don't know! Girls are crazy."

"Go back there and win her over," Jack growls. "Take her out way too late and make her miss work on Saturday when Marlene needs her there. The more you do it, the more she'll want to give up the store."

"That might take a while," Caleb says, sounding more resigned than angry now. "I'm not going to pretend to date this chick, dad. I have a life."

"You'll do what it takes so we can secure the property."

I've heard enough. I'm now so pissed I might be able to

shatter glass with my stare alone. I step into the doorway and reveal myself to the two assholes inside the empty game store.

"Sorry to barge into the party here, but Caleb, I won't be going out with you. Not now, not ever. Lose my number and stop texting me obsessively, you freaking stalker."

His eyes go wide and Jack's face hardens, the lines in his jaw tightening. I don't care. I'm too pissed to care. It's one thing to use me, but no one messes with my mom's store or her happiness.

I level my glare at Caleb's dad. "And you, Mr. Brown, can go piss off. You'll never get my mom's store. I don't care if you buy every store in this town, you won't get hers."

I'm out the door before he can say anything. And they must know what's good for them, because neither one of them chase after me.

24

I'M SO SEETHING MAD I CAN'T GO BACK TO THE STORE JUST YET. Mom will see right through me and she'll obviously think I'm mad about the stupid boy who came to see me. Which I am, but not in the way she thinks. I also don't want to run into Caleb or his stupid dad, so I slip behind the boardwalk to the access hallway where only the janitors and store owners have access. I take some deep breaths and walk back and forth a few times until I feel some of my anger fade away. I'm still pissed, more pissed than I've ever been, but I'm okay now. I am more determined than ever to work at The Magpie now.

I will make it successful and I will open my coffee shop when I'm older.

Back in the store, Mom is sneakily reading that book while standing at the front counter. I roll my eyes at her and begin restocking some greeting cards from the new batch we just had delivered.

"Natalie," Mom says softly. She puts the book on the counter and gives me the exact same look she gave me the day my cat died while I was at school.

"What's wrong?" I say. My hands are now shaking and I

shove them in my back pockets. "I want to talk about something." She pats the stool behind the register. "Come over here."

"Is this about Caleb?" I say as I walk over. "Because I can't stand that guy. He won't be coming back here. I made it very clear I'm not interested in him."

"It's not about boys," she says. She chews on her thumb nail and then it hits me. Mom's not talking slowly because I'm in trouble. She has something she wants to tell me.

Instantly, I panic over the idea that Mom found out I've been talking to my dad's new wife at school. But it's not my fault. She made me talk to her. She's the AP after all. I'm thinking up all these excuses to tell her when she says, "I've been given an offer to sell The Magpie."

I stop just short of sitting on the stool. "Well, who cares about that?" I say. "We're not selling."

Mom's expression isn't exactly comforting. She glances at the counter, probably to avoid looking at me. "It was for fourteen thousand dollars, Natalie. We could survive a few months on that kind of money and I could look for another job. One with benefits and a good salary."

I stand straighter. "Who gave you this offer? And when did it happen?" I've done such a great job of blocking Jack's offers so far.

"A man named Jack Brown," Mom says, and the name makes me flinch even though I'd pretty much expected it. No one else has ever come around here asking to buy us out. She picks up a stack of business cards and straightens them on the counter. "He came by today while you were at school and discussed it with me."

Of course he did. The asshole waited until I was out of the picture and he pounced. If I hadn't been so freaking diligent at going to school lately, maybe I could have been here. I could have stopped it.

"So what?" I say, folding my arms over my chest. "We're not selling. This store is your dream."

"It was my dream with your father," she says, looking down at her hands. "Now that he's gone, I can't exactly use his money to keep us afloat like I used to."

Mom never talks about Dad. Like, never. I close my eyes and exhale. "Tell me you didn't accept his offer."

"Not yet." She grabs my hand and squeezes it. "I said I'd think about it."

"Well call him and say no." I reach for the phone. "I'll do it."

"Natalie." Her voice is stern and I move my hand away from the phone. "We need to think this over."

"I *have* thought it over," I say.

Mom rolls her eyes. "It's only been a few seconds."

Little does she know, I've actually had weeks to think it over from all the times I've intercepted Jack's attempts to talk to my mom. And maybe yesterday I would have considered selling if it made Mom happy, but after the conversation I heard just now in the game store, I refuse to let that asshole win.

"Jack Brown can't buy our store," I say through clenched teeth. "Sell it to someone else if you want, but not him."

"Honey, no one else wants it," she says with a sigh. "I'm not saying I'm happy about the idea of selling, but maybe this is what we need. Money has been tight for so long now and I just want to breathe again."

"But this is your dream." I point to the other side of the store. "And that's going to be my coffee shop one day. I'll go to college soon and I'll get my degree and open the store."

"College is four years away," she says.

"So what? I'll get a two year associates degree in business at the community college. I'll be close enough to keep working here and then I'll open my coffee shop and finish out two more years of college."

"Honey..." I know what she's thinking, that opening a business *and* going to school is pretty much impossible. But I don't care right now.

"We can't sell to that asshole."

"Honey," she says again, this time with a warning in her voice.

I grab my backpack from under the counter, knowing I need to get out of here before I lose my mind. "I refuse to let you sell the store," I tell her as I sling it on my back. "You of all people know how important small businesses are. If you let the Jack Browns of the world buy up everything, then that'll all be gone. He'll be more of a rich asshole and the little guys will lose."

This hits home, I know it. Her eyes widen in recognition and I know I've struck a nerve with her and her love of small businesses.

"I'm going home to work on homework," I tell her. "And you can stay here and think about what a terrible idea it would be to sell this place."

Mom and I both know the best thing for me to do is to hang out at the store for another hour until it closes and she can take me home in her car. But the fact that I walk right out, ready to trudge home in the summer heat with my heavy backpack instead of being with her one more minute should hopefully prove my point. My mom needs the time alone. She needs to remember what this store means to her. And I need some time to come up with a better plan than simply begging Mom to turn away Jack's offer.

If I wasn't stuck going to school every day, then I'd have more time to spend trying to drum up business. I haven't even updated the store's Facebook page in a week because I've been too busy trying to pass my classes. Well, that's not good enough. I need to work harder. I need to save this freaking store.

When I get home, it's almost six o'clock and I'm drenched in sweat. I take a quick shower and then plop on my bed, too exhausted and pissed off to do any of my extra credit worksheets.

My heart aches for Jonah, for his warmth and his smile and a hug. He would make me feel better if he were here right now, but since Mom will be home soon and the tension between us is so high, I can't invite him over. Instead, I'll have to settle for the next best thing.

Me: Can I call you?

The phone rings a few seconds after I send the text. "If you want to call me, just call me," Jonah says. "You don't have to text me first."

"I didn't know if you were busy," I say as I sit on my bed and stare out the window.

"I'm never too busy to talk to you. What's up?"

I sigh. "How much time do you have?"

"As much time as you need," he says with a smile in his voice.

I tell him about the store, and how we've been suffering with money lately, which he already knows. Then I tell him about stupid Jack Brown and all his previous inquiries about buying The Magpie and how I blocked them. Jonah balks when I tell him Jack's offer price.

"Surely the store is worth more than that," he says. "Typically businesses sell for twice the yearly profit. His offer is an insult."

"He's offering low because he doesn't want the business. He just wants to strip the space clean and make it another one of his office buildings. Jack Brown doesn't care about anything but himself."

"So what does your mom say?" he asks.

"That's the worst part, Jonah. I think she's actually considering it."

"Don't stress, chica. It'll be okay."

"It won't be okay," I say. I bite my lip but I know he needs to know the real truth. "We can't sell the store to Jack Brown. Then he would have won."

"Won what?" Jonah asks.

As much as I hate this, I want Jonah to know the truth so that there are no secrets between us. I feel like a total idiot, but I go ahead and tell him about Caleb, and how his dad made him talk to me in an effort to get our store. Jonah listens, and I can practically hear the gears in his brain turning as he takes in all of this new information.

"So what's why we can't sell to him," I say, my heart heavy with regret and anger. "If Mom wants to sell to someone else, I could probably be okay with it, but we can't sell to Jack. He can't win."

"No, he can't," Jonah says. "That's why we're going to save your store. We're going to make The Magpie so freaking profitable that your mom will never sell it to anyone."

"How are we going to do that?" I say.

Jonah takes a breath. The phone shuffles, and I hear a page flip over in his notebook. "We're going to come up with a plan."

25

JONAH AND I SPENT THE REST OF THE NIGHT TALKING ON THE phone and coming up with ideas to save the store. There's no magic trick to success here. Basically, we need to do exactly what I've been trying to do all year—earn more money. Get more sales. Find more customers. Spread the word.

I told Jonah there's just no other option because I've tried them all, but he refused to believe that. He's taken some free business classes at the local community college just for fun over his summer breaks, and he thinks that'll help him find ways to generate more income. He swears he has new ideas for us to try, but we'll need a few days for him to figure them out and make an official plan. That's the difference with Jonah and me. I just go for it, trying out ideas randomly. He makes a plan. He's probably typing up a spreadsheet before school starts.

When I meet with April the next morning for our walk to school, I don't even know how to start telling her all the stuff she missed. The talk with Caleb, his obsessive texts, and the explosion with his dad. The offer to buy our business and most of all – the kiss. The glorious kiss I shared with Jonah.

As soon as I see her I smile and want to dive into telling her everything, but then my tongue gets stuck in my mouth. It's just too much information to process right now.

"How's your head?" I ask her.

"Finally better." She makes this exhausted face and presses her palm to her forehead. "The migraines are the worst pain ever, and the drugs they give me for them aren't much better. It takes away some of the pain, but it makes my body all warm and tingly. Feels like I'm sunburned all over."

"Well, I'm glad to have you back," I say as we walk.

"Did you actually go to school yesterday without me or did you ditch?" She eyes me suspiciously, probably trying to figure out if I'm lying or not.

Before I got busted by the AP, anytime April was sick or had a migraine, I didn't bother going to school either. My reasoning was that it's boring to walk alone and it's also horrible to eat lunch in the cafeteria alone. Sure, I have some old friends from my junior year that I could probably sit with, but they've all pretty much ditched me since last summer when I dedicated all my time to the store. Plus, skipping school has always meant more time at the store.

I put my hands on my hips. "I'll have you know, I went to school. And I went to every single class, and I actually did all my work, too."

"Wow," she says, her eyes going wide. "I can't believe you're taking this all so seriously. I mean, I'm glad you are, but when they set you up with that detention plan I just knew you'd blow it off."

I shrug. "I really want to graduate. Plus, now I want Jonah's tutoring to be appreciated." I toss my hands in the air. "So what can I do? I have to go."

"You and Jonah," she says wistfully. "When are you going to finally admit to liking him?"

"Well..." I bite my lip and look over at her. We stop at an

intersection. April puts a hand on her hip. "Well what? Don't tell me you're still in denial here."

"I'm about as far from denial as you can get," I tell her, unable to hide my grin.

"What does that mean?"

"It means we kissed."

"You WHAT?" April grabs both of my arms and jumps up and down, oblivious to the traffic around us, mostly students who go to our school and can totally see us standing here looking like idiots.

"I need details!" she shrieks in a rare show of crazy emotion.

I start laughing and then I'm bouncing on my toes too. "I kissed him!"

"You kissed him!"

"Also, I told Caleb's dad to piss off."

April stops bouncing. "What happened when I was gone yesterday?"

I hold onto my backpack straps and take a deep breath. The school is just up ahead and we always stop talking about personal things by the time we cross this road so that no one overhears us. "It's a long story. A crazy long story that might involve losing The Magpie."

April's eyebrows pull together. "You're kidding."

I shake my head. "I wish. I'll have to tell you during lunch, okay?"

"No way. No freaking way." April grabs my elbow and tugs me toward the right, turning onto Main Street. "We're getting coffee," she says as she picks up speed.

"But...first period?" I say, but I walk alongside her. "The bell rings in ten minutes."

"It can wait."

If she wants to ditch class for some Starbucks down the road, I'm perfectly okay with that. I've been a model student for the last month. I can screw up one class period.

The moment we place our coffee orders, Jonah texts me.

Jonah: I have some preliminary plans for The Magpie. Want me to give them to you now so you can look over before we talk at lunch?

Me: I'm not at school…I'm at Starbucks.

Me: Please don't be mad!

Jonah: Why'd you skip?

Me: I told April a very brief description of what happened while she was sick and she's dying for details.

Jonah: Cool. Can I come?

I tilt my phone to April and let her read his text. "Absolutely," she says, taking my phone from my hand and texting that word back to him. "I want to hear all about the hanky-panky you two have been up to while I was gone."

We sit at a table in the corner that has a view of the window facing the school, just in case any teachers or principals decide to come in here looking for students who are skipping. Jonah shows up a few minutes later, his hair a little messy from the wind.

"Hey," he says, sliding into the chair next to me. He gives me a quick kiss on the cheek and I blush from head to toe.

April grins. "Spill your guts, kids. I need details!"

After Jonah assures me he doesn't mind missing first period, we all make a promise to talk just for this hour and then get back to school for second period. Missing one measly math class shouldn't have Mrs. Reese freaking out or anything. I'll say I was sick and needed to come into school late, or blame it on cramps.

I start with the beginning, and tell April everything that happened yesterday. I kind of skim over the romantic parts of the day with Jonah because I don't want to give away all of our special moments to other people. Jonah helps me tell the story in places, and when we're done, April is just as pissed off as I am about Jack Brown's offer to buy the store and the sleazy way he tried to get his son to win me over.

"So although I fear this is hopeless and totally won't work," I say, eyeing Jonah who gives me a reassuring smile, "Jonah thinks we can come up with a plan to save the store."

"Damn right we can." He places his notebook on the table. To my surprise, he hasn't concocted a spreadsheet on the computer or anything, he's just written a ton of stuff in his super small but very neat handwriting.

"We're going to do a community outreach," Jonah says. "Most of the store's business is from tourists and beach goers, but how many citizens of Sterling bother to go shopping on the boardwalk on a daily basis? Not many." He taps the paper. "We're going to bring the whole town to you. The Magpie will become a place to stop for all of your gift-giving, book-buying, trinket-desiring needs. We'll have a book club, and student discounts, and social media campaigns. It's going to be great."

I study over his ideas, many of which I've never thought of myself. They're also really good. April throws in some ideas as well, and Jonah adds them to the list.

When we're all coffee-d up and walking back to school, I get a text.

Mom: Sorry babe. I've decided to sell the store.

"No!" My hands tremble and tears flood my eyes.

"What is it?" Jonah says, his hand on my back. "Who texted?"

"My mother," I say as a tear falls down my cheek. Just minutes ago, I'd been so happy and hopeful for the store. Now that dream is crushed. "She wants to sell." I show them the text and April and Jonah are stunned into silence, which only makes me cry harder.

Then Jonah takes the phone from me and presses the call button over my mom's name. "Talk to her," he says, pushing the phone back to me. "Tell her to give it three more months.

Promise her the store will earn at least a thousand extra dollars a month and if it does, she'll reconsider."

I nod quickly, trying to remember everything he just said, even though I'm pretty sure it's hopeless. We've lost and Jack Brown has won. Mom answers the phone after several rings, probably because she wasn't sure if she wanted to answer knowing I'd probably be mad.

"You can't sell the store," I say.

"Natalie—" Mom begins. "We've been over this."

"Yes, but I've got a proposition for you. Tell Jack you need three months to decide."

"Nat—"

"Tell him. He'll wait. He has no other choice. And in these next three months, I'll have the store earning a thousand dollars more per month. No—fifteen hundred," I say. Jonah's eyes widen, but he nods.

"Please, Mom." I grip the phone to my ear as a tear rolls down my cheek. "Please believe in me. If it doesn't work out in three months, you can sell the store with my blessing."

"Fine," Mom says after a long moment of silence. "You have a deal."

26

A nervous energy flows through my veins on Saturday morning. It's as if my body knows something bad is about to happen, but it won't tell me what. I get up and get dressed way earlier than usual because Jonah is going to meet me at The Magpie an hour before we open so we can start on our plan to earn more money. Fifteen hundred dollars spread out over a month is only fifty dollars a day that we need to earn above what we normally earn. It sounds simple, maybe even easy, but I know how many days I've spent at The Magpie when not a single customer has even walked through our door. Fifty dollars is a lot.

I brush my teeth, still unable to shake that feeling of dread. When I get to the kitchen, the smell of coffee isn't filling the room like usual. Mom sits at the table, reading news on her tablet.

"Good morning," I say. "Are we out of coffee?"

"I just didn't feel like making it." Mom's eyes stay focused on the tablet. I grab some Pop Tarts from the pantry and sit next to her. Although I'd love some coffee, I don't really have time to make a fresh pot right now since Jonah will be here to pick me up in a few minutes.

"Are you okay?" I ask my mom after a few minutes of silence. She's staring at her tablet, but she's not focusing on anything. With my question hanging in the air, she looks up at me.

Oh no. This is not a good look.

"About what I agreed to yesterday," Mom says, still not looking at me. "I can't do ninety days. I'll do thirty days."

The knot in my stomach seems to look up at me and say *this is why I made you wake up feeling sick.*

I take a deep breath and try not to lash out and cry and beg for what I want. "Why not three months?" I ask calmly. "You know business things take a while."

She nods. "Try sixteen years. I have been there done that, Natalie. Even if we do a few things to the store, it doesn't bring about long term change."

"But it will," I say. "Jonah is going to help me and he's incredibly smart."

Mom snorts. "Right. A kid in high school will do better than a team of market researchers that I hired a couple years ago."

"He might," I say, breaking off a piece of my Pop Tart. "He's crazy smart and he already has a ton of ideas. He'll be here any minute and we're heading to the store to start working on them."

Mom shakes her head like she still thinks I'm stupid for giving even one ounce of hope to Jonah's plans. "You can have thirty more days to play with the store, and then I'm selling."

Maybe she's given up, but I'm not. "Okay. Fine. I'll change your mind over the next thirty days."

"Well, have fun," she says as she looks back at her tablet. "I won't be going into work this weekend. I need a break."

Jonah hands me a Starbucks frap when I climb into his car. I grab it with wide eyes and clutch it to my chest. "You are amazing," I say, taking a sip. "My hero."

He laughs. "Is your mom okay with me hanging out at the store all day?"

"She's not going to be there at all," I tell him, the words feeling awkward as they leave my mouth. "She's never taken off work unless she was really sick. Also, she's only giving me thirty days, so I'm not sure how we'll change her mind in that short of a time span."

Jonah puts a hand on my knee and gives me one of his classic reassuring smiles. "We will. My mom's annoying book club friends are coming over today to shop, and we have a meeting with Sue Cho at two."

"A meeting?" I say, giving him a look. "Isn't Sue Cho the name of a girl at school?"

"She's the student council president," he says, wiggling his eyebrows at me as if he just introduced me to a celebrity.

"Okay...?"

We've arrived at the store, so he walks over to my side and slides his arm around my waist. "Just trust me. I'll explain it all in the meeting."

Jonah's mom is tall and beautiful, with long silky black hair and tanned skin a little darker than Jonah's. They have the same eyes, but Jonah must have gotten a lot of his features from his dad. She arrives around eleven after having brunch with the seven women in her book club. Jonah introduces me to her and I mumble over a hello instead of being suave and charming like I'd tried to be.

All eight women have a lively discussion in front of our bookshelves while they decide which book to buy for this coming week's club meeting.

After choosing a mystery novel, Mrs. Garza asks if we'd be able to order any book they want in advance.

"Yes, absolutely," I say. "We can order any book online."

"Wonderful. We'd like to use your store as our weekly book supplier."

"You have book clubs weekly?" I ask, eyebrows raised. All the book clubs I've ever known take a month to read a book.

"Of course." She glances at Jonah and smiles at him the way moms always smile at the children they love. "The best way to live is by reading at least one book a week." She hefts four different hardbacks onto the counter. "These are just for my personal reading," she says, giving me a grin. "I tend to read more than the other women do."

"Thank you so much for shopping here," I say loud enough for all the book club ladies to hear. "I'm so glad to help you all. Are these separate orders or all together?"

"Separate, dear," a short woman with a Botox face says. "But we're not nearly finished shopping yet. Can you hold these up front for us?"

"Of course." I stack their books on the counter in eight piles. Just like Jonah's mom had done, every other woman buys at least one more book. I look over at Jonah and he winks at me.

"These are the women you need shopping in your store. Most of them don't work and have wealthy husbands. And, none of them have never been here before. They didn't know it existed."

"This is awesome," I say, mentally adding up how much profit we'll earn on around thirty book sales. "But unless your mom has a different book club with hundreds of other women each week, this won't help us much in the long term."

"No, but everything put together will." Jonah wiggles the mouse on the computer. "How do I log in here?"

I log him into the store's account and he goes to the website for the software we use to keep track of inventory and purchases.

"Whatcha doing?" I ask over his shoulder. I can't help but inhale the sweet clean scent of him and I hope he doesn't notice.

"I want to kiss you so bad right now," he says in a low whisper. "My mother better leave soon."

I slap him playfully on the back. "I want them to stay a long time and buy lots of stuff," I whisper back.

"I see how it is… money is more important than kissing me." He turns around and grins at me and we're standing so close my boobs slide against his arm.

"That's not a fair question," I whisper back. My lips are tingling with the desire to lift up on my toes and kiss him, but that won't happen with his mom just a few feet away. I need to be professional so I can secure these women as repeat customers.

Jonah clears his throat and I notice his ears are red. He turns back to the computer and I press up against his back, leaning to the side to see what he's doing.

"Your point of sale software comes with a free add on download for customer loyalty. As I suspected, you don't have that option set up here yet."

"What is it for?" I ask.

He clicks around on the website and then a downloading box appears. "You input the customer's phone number each time they purchase something. After a certain amount of purchases, they get a reward. Like the stamp cards at the frozen yogurt place."

"Awesome," I say, watching as he installs and sets up the loyalty program. It appears as a little button we can click as we ring up a customer.

We set it up so that every ten purchases gives you a coupon for twenty percent off your next order. Then Jonah and I set up an announcement to let everyone know about our new loyally program on the store's website, Facebook page, and mailing list.

When Mrs. Garza and her friends are done shopping, they each have a ton of items they can't stop raving about. I ring them each up, putting them in the loyalty program which really delights them. As I work, they talk to each other about the cute items we stock, and the books, and how they need to come back and with their other friends to show them around this store, which they all agree is "very cute."

I'm beaming with pride as I swipe credit card after credit card while Jonah bags their items. I still don't know if I can turn this place around in thirty days, but at least I'm not going down without a fight.

The moment the door closes behind the last one of Jonah's mom's friends, he turns to me. His eyes narrow slightly and he grabs onto my hips, pulling me closer to him. "You are really sexy," he says, lowering his forehead to mine.

"In these clothes?" I say, pulling at the front of my Magpie polo shirt.

"In any clothes," he whispers. My toes tingle at his nearness, the warmth of his hands on my sides. I lean up and finally let myself do what I've wanted to do all morning.

His kiss is slow and passionate, his tongue gliding over my lips slowly until I part them. And then we kiss harder, our tongues sliding across each other in ways that make my whole body light up. My hands wrap around his neck and his dig into my sides, tugging me so close our bodies are pressed against each other from shoulders to knees.

I can feel his bulge press against my leg and it turns me on knowing he's turned on. His hands slide up my sides, his thumbs grazing under the cup of my bra. I gasp for air and then go in to kiss him again, wishing his lips were all over me, in every place that tingles with desire.

His thumbs slide across my breasts and then he glides down my sides until his thumbs find a resting place just inside the waistband of my jeans. I am warm and hot and tingling for his touch. I slide my fingers through the back of his hair, moaning when he kisses my neck. He chuckles at this, the sound soft and playful, before he kisses another trail from my collar bone back up to my mouth, his body slowly grinding against mine in ways that make me want to rip these stupid clothes off.

It's hard to imagine that the boy with clean cut clothes and a dorky messenger bag at school would be so unbelievably great at making out. There are hidden treasures beneath guys who don't flaunt themselves like sex gods on the football field. And I've just found one.

Jonah leans my back against the counter, his erection pressing against my belly button. I let out a sigh of pleasure as I pull him closer to me, sliding my hands under his shirt to feel the skin I've only seen once at the beach. I'm about to take it too far, but I don't care, not one bit.

And then the phone rings.

I jump at the sudden high pitched sound and Jonah steps backward, blinking his eyes as if returning from a daze.

"Whoa," he says, breathing heavily. He reaches into his back pocket and takes out his phone. "We have to answer this." He gives me a devilish grin and then leans forward and kisses me one slow, delicious time before answering the call.

I have to take several deep breaths before I can focus on the conversation, but the gist of it is that Sue Cho has chosen The Magpie as this year's school fundraiser store. All we have to do is agree to donate ten percent of our profits to the school for everyone who comes in and turns in a Student Council fundraiser coupon.

Jonah describes it as a win/win deal because the school earns money, which we can call a tax deduction for the store, and more people come into the store because their kids bring home coupons encouraging them to.

We agree to get started right away, and Sue sends out an email to the elementary school administration, telling them we're on board to sponsor every school in the district, not just the high school. One of the principals calls the store directly an hour later and asks if they can send out a code to parents via email instead of a coupon so that we can save paper and be environmentally friendly.

I think up a code word and by the end of the day, we've brought in eight hundred dollars of sales, one hundred of which we're donating to the school.

It's only day one, I think as we prepare to lock up the store after closing. And we're already mostly there.

27

Mom has slipped back into her depression again. She spends the whole weekend at home while I run the store with Jonah and April's help. The Student Council fundraising thing is going really well so far, and we close out Sunday night with two thousand extra dollars in sales. I'm thrilled to come home and tell my mom, but when I find her in her room, laid on her side and staring at the wall, I can't think of anything to say.

Mom gets like this sometimes. It doesn't happen often, but it's happened mostly after she got divorced. She'll go through a few days of silent contemplation and she won't leave her room much or do anything. I know she's upset right now because of her decision to sell the store, and I know it's a battle I can't win right now.

If we can do two thousand dollars in sales on a weekend, I can only imagine how much we'll earn over the next twenty-eight days. I make a BLT sandwich with chips and set it on a tray, then take it to Mom's room. I set it on her nightstand and then turn to walk away.

"Thank you," she says.

After a shower, I'm sitting in my room working on my extra

credit papers and trying not to worry about Mom. With Jonah's help, we might actually turn this place around. The weird thing is that I know we've earned around three thousand dollars a month for the last few months. Sure we have taxes and rent to pay, but besides the normal bills and food and stuff, we shouldn't need any more money than that. We're barely getting by here, but at least we're getting by, right? Mom and I live without cable TV or high speed internet and we get by just fine. Why is she so quick to give this all up and get a job that she'll hate?

Frustrated and feeling a little depressed myself, I shove my homework to the side and head down to the kitchen nook where Mom keeps all her bills and mail. I grab a notepad and smile when it makes me think of Jonah, and then I write Monthly Budget at the top.

I grab a stack of the latest bills and start writing down the electric company, water company, and cell phone provider, along with what last month's bill amount was for each one. I'm going to figure out what it costs to survive each month and then see if I can tweak the budget to save money.

With money saved and more money coming into the store, Mom will have to reconsider the idea of selling the store. I'll beg and plead. I'll do whatever it takes to keep the store in my life and make sure Jack Brown doesn't get his way.

I go through the bills and find Mom's bank account statement for last month. I figure I'll add up all the food and grocery expenses to see what we spend on food on average. Surely, we can budget better in that area by eating cheap food and cutting out smoothies and ice cream.

I get halfway down the page when my finger stops on a transaction I don't recognize. Twelve hundred dollars was paid to EASYMONEYCORP.

I sit back and stare at the numbers on the bank statement. Easy Money Corp? That payday loan place that's always advertising on the radio? Why is Mom paying them so much money?

I go back to the bills and flip through each one, not seeing anything from this shady payday loan place. Then I remember when I was little and how Mom would hide her favorite candy from me so I'd stop eating it all in one sitting. Would Mom hide something from me now?

I shove the chair over to the fridge, where I stand on it to look into the shoebox that's been up there forever, collecting dust. There's no candy in it anymore, but there is paperwork. Lots of it.

Half an hour later, my heart is pounding and I'm freaking out. My mom took a payday loan last year around Christmas time. It must have been what she used to buy my new cell phone even though I'd told her we didn't need to waste money on things like that. The interest they charge on this loan is impossible and Mom's monthly payments keep going up and up each month, especially since she took out a few more loans after the first one.

Now my mom owes $23,557 and the monthly payment is $1206. They call it the minimum payment and there's a line on the bill encouraging you to pay more. Each month $800 is added on in interest. It makes me want to throw up. This should be illegal. They're taking advantage of my poor mom who only wanted a little extra cash to get us by. This is ruining us. No wonder she kept it a secret.

I shove everything back in place, grab the monthly budget I'd made and go back to my room where I call Jonah.

"Hello?" he says all groggily.

"Did I wake you up?" I look at my watch—it's after midnight. "I'm so sorry."

"It's okay. What's up?"

I tell him about all of the debt my mom has secretly acquired and how it's with a shady company. Even with the extra money we've earned last weekend, it won't be enough. That barely covers a payment and the high interest will just keep the debt at the same amount. I hope Jonah has a plan. Some fancy mathematical way to make this easier to pay off.

He tells me we're screwed. That payday loans are sharks and they bankrupt people more often than they help them. He says there's no way out of this loan without a lump sum payment of the full amount.

We can do what we can for the store, but we'll never get twenty thousand dollars.

ALL I WANT TO DO IS SKIP CLASS ON MONDAY, BUT I FORCE myself to go. Mom seemed okay, more like her usual self this morning. At least she was going to the store and not choosing to close for the day so she can stay in bed. I wanted to tell her about the loan and how I knew about it, but I don't want to upset her. I want to fix this. If only that debt was paid off, then we could keep the store.

Jonah meets me in the hallway on the way to lunch, his hand slipping into mine as if it were created specifically for that purpose. "How you holding up?" he asks.

I lean against his arm while we walk. "I don't know. I wish Mom would have told me about this."

"Parents don't want their kids to worry."

"Yeah, well now I'm worrying."

Jonah tugs my hand in the opposite direction of the cafeteria. I let him guide me back the way we came, walking against the flow of traffic, until we get to the alcove underneath the stairs.

He glances around suspiciously, and when the last student has left this hallway, he pulls me inside.

"Jonah," I say playfully as I press his back to the wall and lean against him. "You're a world class student. Sneaking around at school doesn't sound like you at all."

"I know," he says, sliding his hands in my back pockets. There's a hint of mischief in his eyes as we kiss. "We can't stay here long, I just had to get a kiss and tell you how crazy I am about you."

"Let's get to it then," I say. I reach up and cup his face in my hands. Then I lean on my toes and let my body fall against his chest, my lips crashing into his. We kiss just enough to enjoy it but not enough to get too turned on. We're at school, after all.

"Now I believe you had something to tell me," I say with a coy grin.

"I am crazy about you," he says, holding me tightly.

"The feeling is mutual," I say, leaning against his chest. "Thanks for cheering me up."

"That's what boyfriends do."

I look up at him. "Are you saying you're my boyfriend?"

He gazes into my eyes. "Do you want me to be?"

I'm suddenly nervous, jittery, and feeling like I'm not good enough for all of this wonderful boy. I can't find the words to say yes, so I nod.

He smiles and kisses me again. "We're official now."

"I like the sound of that," I say, taking his hand and stepping back into the hallway. "Official."

Someone calls my name. I don't recognize the girl who rushes up to me, out of breath. "There you are," she says, holding out a piece of paper. "I've been looking all over for you."

I take the paper. It's pink. It has the AP's office checked at the top. All those happy feelings I'd had with Jonah just seconds ago vanish. They're taken away, sliced in half with this piece of paper that's making me go see that woman again.

I turn to Jonah. "Tell April I'll probably miss lunch."

He frowns and pulls me into a hug. "Good luck."

Mrs. Reese doesn't make me wait outside her office forever

like she did last time. She ushers me right in, telling me to sit. She's smiling and talking in a kind voice, so maybe she's in a good mood. I'm still not very thrilled with being here.

There's a picture on her desk of her and my ex stepdad, their faces leaning toward each other on a roller coaster ride.

"What can I do for you?" I say.

"Just wanted to have an update, Natalie." Mrs. Reese beams at me and looks at her computer screen. "You now have four B's, two A's, and only one C on this report card. I am so very proud of you."

"What can I say, the tutoring helped."

Her smile shifts into one less convincing. "Natalie, I spoke with a few of your teachers this morning and they all said you seemed upset about something. Can I ask what's bothering you?"

"It's nothing school related," I say, waving her off with my hand. "Just a little disappointed that my mom wants to sell the store."

"Why would she do that?" Mrs. Reese says, her voice softening as if she's talking about a friend instead of her husband's ex-wife.

I shrug. "We're not making enough money."

She leans forward and takes a pen, then writes something on a small notepad. "You should talk to your dad," she says, sliding the paper to me. It contains a phone number and an email address. "He could help you."

"I'm not asking my mom's ex-husband for money," I say, shoving the paper back across her desk.

"Honey—" Frown lines form around her mouth and then she tries to smile at me. "Don't think of him like that. Think of him as your adopted dad. He cares a lot about you, Natalie."

"He doesn't call me. He hasn't emailed or written or seen me at all."

"That's because you told him not to."

I flinch. "What? No I didn't."

Her eyes flicker with something unreadable, and then she frowns again. She slides the paper back to me. "Maybe you should reach out and let him know there's been a misunderstanding."

"Did my mom tell him I don't want to see him?" I ask. My throat feels dry and I try to think of a world where Mom did that to me. Of course, she also lied to me about having major debt, so maybe she did this as well.

"I don't have the answers, Natalie. But I do know your dad has a college fund set up for you. He has child support he wanted to pay but your mom wouldn't accept."

I swallow. "Are you serious?"

She nods slowly, pity all over her face. "He misses you."

"I don't want money from him."

"That's fine." She pushes the paper closer to my hand. "Maybe just a phone call. I know he would be so happy to hear from you."

28

"Your mom looks better," Jonah says.

"What?" I look up from my phone, where I'd been posting stuff to the store's Facebook page. Jonah is driving me home and he should have no idea what my mom looks like since she's at home, and in bed, I'd assume.

Then I see her sitting on the porch, a cup of coffee in her hand even though it's eight in the evening. She's dressed, which is unusual. When I left her this morning, she was in her bathrobe and looked ready to spend all day in bed. Now she's wearing her nice jeans that only come out of the closet occasionally, and a pink top that's been ironed since I last saw it. Her hair is brushed, maybe even curled at the tips. She waves at us as Jonah pulls into my driveway.

"Er," I say, biting on my bottom lip as I look at my boyfriend. "Can you maybe just drop me off and leave? I'm sorry...I ... I just don't want to introduce you to her now."

He chuckles and reaches over and squeezes my hand. "No problem, Nat. You don't have to introduce me until you're ready."

"You're such an amazing boyfriend," I say, my face falling

into a pout because I can't kiss him, not with my mom watching. "Pretend I'm kissing you right now."

He closes his eyes for a second. "Wow, chica. That was dirty." He wiggles his eyebrows. "I didn't know you liked to kiss that way…"

I punch him playfully in the arm and get out of his car.

"Hey…Mom," I say as I walk up to the porch. I'm not sure if I should keep it casual or ask why she's dressed so nice when she couldn't bother coming to work today. We could have used her help with all the extra customers.

"Sit down, honey." Mom pats the dirty wooden step next to her. We should really power wash these porch steps one day. I sit, the smell of her coffee wafting in my direction. She takes a sip.

"Jack Brown has increased his offer to fifteen thousand dollars, plus I will have two weeks to remove and keep all of the inventory."

My fingers tremble, so I shove them under my thighs and sit on them to keep still. "Okay…"

She gives me a soft smile. "That's pretty much unheard of in business, Natalie. When someone buys a business, they're buying the whole thing. So this offer…well it's quite a bit more because we have at least ten, maybe fifteen thousand dollars of inventory."

"So what would you do with it?" I ask, trying to play along until I find the right moment to tell her about our profits today.

"I'd sell it online. I think we could box it up and fit it all in the living room, maybe some of it in my room if there's not enough space. I can spend a week or two listing everything for sale, and that will be my full time job until we've sold most of it. Jack will even let me keep the business name, so we can change our website and social media accounts to say that The Magpie is now an online store."

I don't even know what to think about this. I take a deep breath. "So that's what you'd do? Run a business online?"

She shakes her head and takes a long sip of coffee. "Not exactly. You can't make a good living like that. I'd just sell off the inventory to get the value of it. Maybe sell some stuff in a big lot at a discount. I don't know... I just want to get the value of the items back. Then I'd have to get a job."

Okay, Natalie. Be logical so she listens to you.

I clear my throat. "Mom...that is a good idea," I say against everything in my heart screaming *no it isn't!* "However...fifteen thousand dollars isn't much to live on for very long and then you'd still have the pressure of finding a job...maybe we should give The Magpie a chance. It hasn't even been thirty days yet and—"

"Natalie, I'm selling." Mom's lips flatten and she gives me one of her looks, the classic Mom look that says I better shut up or I'll get in trouble.

"But..."

Her eyes widen. "No buts, Natalie. I am the adult and you're still a child. I make the decisions, and I'm selling."

I grit my teeth as fear rockets through me. I can't lose this store. "Mom! Why? That shouldn't be enough money to make you give up on your dream. This store is our life."

"We'll make another life," she says, looking away just as I think I see a tear form in her eyes. "Don't bother arguing. You don't understand, but we need that money."

"I do understand, Mom." I stand up. "I saw your debt. I know about the payday loan."

Mom's eyes flash with anger and then she looks down at her feet. "Well then you know how badly I need this money," she says so quietly I almost don't hear her.

"Mom..." I sit back down, put a hand on her shoulder. "We made a lot of money at the store today. We have all of the local schools telling parents to come shop with us. We will keep working until we get that loan paid off."

She shakes her head. "You can't pay it off. You'd need a ton of money and we'll never make that much at the store."

"You can't just give up, Mom!"

Now she stands. She grips the coffee mug so hard in her hand, it might shatter. "Yes. I. Can. I am the mother and I can do whenever I feel it's best for our well-being."

A tear rolls down her cheek and I wish I was smart enough to think of exactly the right words to change her mind. "Mom… We don't have to sell the store. We can find a way to pay off the debt."

"No, we can't," she snaps. "We need over twenty thousand dollars to pay it off and we'll never get that without selling. I'm sorry, but it's over. I'm signing the papers next week."

She storms into the house, the door slamming closed behind her. I rest my elbows on my knees and stare out at the front yard as tears slide down my face and splash onto the stairs below.

IT'S LATE. TOO LATE. I KNOW THIS, AND I SHOULD TURN BACK around and pedal my bike back home. But here I am, riding through town just a little before midnight on a school night. Jonah said he lives on 4th Street, and that's where I decided to go when I couldn't sleep.

I feel like a stalker as I ride my bike slowly down the middle of the road, checking each house on both sides, looking for his car.

It doesn't take long to find it parked at the end of a driveway. Jonah's house is big. So big you could probably fit three of my own inside of it and still have room to live in. It's two stories tall and red brick with white shutters. I park my bike behind his car and send him a text.

Me: are you awake?

Jonah: Yes, what's up?

Me: I can't sleep

Jonah: What did your mom say when you got home?

I still haven't told him. Now I don't think I can text it. Saying the words means admitting the truth; that I've failed myself, my mom, and the store.

I must take too long to reply because my phone starts ringing, and I hadn't turned off the sound so it blasts this dark street with what feels like the loudest ring in the world. I quickly answer the phone.

"Hello?"

"Why are you whispering?" Jonah says.

My heart skips a beat as I realize how pathetic this is. I biked over to a guy's house without being invited. He never even gave me his address. Way to be a weirdo, Natalie.

"Um...I don't... I'm outside."

"Outside? Is anyone with you?"

"Technically, no..."

"Natalie...what's going on? Are you okay?"

I sigh. This is embarrassing, but I really want to see him. "I couldn't sleep so I got on my bike and the next thing I know, I'm on 4th Street and—it was totally a coincidence—"

"Are you at my house?" To my relief, he doesn't sound like he's creeped out. If anything, he sounds excited.

"Sort of."

A light turns on upstairs. I watch the curtains, waiting to see Jonah look out of them, but instead, I see a shadowy figure approaching from the side of the house a few moments later.

I hang up the phone as Jonah comes into view. He's wearing black boxers with little dog bones on them and no shirt or shoes. My pulse quickens when he pulls me into a hug, wrapping his arms around me. His body is warm, his skin soft, and he smells like a fresh shower.

"Let's get inside," he whispers as he kisses the side of my head. "Then you can tell me everything."

Jonah's house smells really good, like a mixture of laundry detergent and vanilla candles. It's dark, too dark to see much, so I let him hold my hand and lead me through his house to the stairs, which are covered in thick carpet that masks the sound of our footsteps.

He takes me to his room and closes and locks the door behind us. "Just so no one walks in here and sees a girl in my room," he explains.

And then his arms are around me again, and I'm sliding my hands across his bare back, pressing my face against his chest. I breathe in deeply, feeling at peace for the first time all night.

Jonah takes me to his bed in the sweetest way. I'm not worried he'll try to do something I'm not ready for. I feel safe here, laying in his arms.

While we lay on his bed, cuddled up in each other, I tell him about the store and my mom's newest declaration that she's selling it no matter what. And then, because I can't help but want to tell Jonah everything about everything, I tell him about the assistant principal and her connection to my dad.

"You think your mom told him you don't want to talk to him?" he asks.

I nod as I watch his fingers trace circles on my arm. "I never really got to talk to him after they split up. He was just gone. My mom acted like he left us, like he was just another deadbeat asshole like my biological father."

"Did you ever try to talk to him?" Jonah asks.

I shake my head. "No."

"Maybe you should."

"I mean…" I exhale. "I'm fine without him. But sometimes I

do miss him, you know? He was basically my dad, even though he wasn't really related to me."

"Well…" Jonah's fingers slide under my chin and pull up slightly so he can kiss me. "You could send him an email. It's less personal and not as difficult as meeting or talking on the phone. Then just see where it goes from there."

I shake my head while I look into his eyes, my thoughts now on Jonah's lips and not the idea of emails to a dad I haven't seen in three years. "I don't know," I say. "It's just so awkward."

"Maybe think it over a few days."

I nod, agreeing with him, and then when I can't take it anymore, I slide my hand across his chest and lean over, kissing his neck.

His breath hitches, his hands sliding down to my hips. In a quick movement, I am pulled up from the bed, and now I'm on top of him, his hands gripping my hips, a smirk on his lips.

"That's more like it," he says, lifting his head off the pillow to kiss me.

I straddle him, resting my knees on the bed with my hands on either side of his head. I lean forward and kiss him, letting our mouths fall into the make out routine we're so good at. I revel in the feel of his hands sliding under my shirt and up my back, then down again until they slide over my butt. He squeezes it, grinning against my kiss and then he rocks his hips against mine. It all feels amazing, but my heart is pounding so hard I'm sure the people across the street can hear it.

I lift up, breaking our kiss. "Jonah," I breathe, wondering when it was that I lost my breath during this make out session. "I'm not sure how far I want to take things right now."

"No rush, chica," he whispers against my lips. "We have all the time in the world."

29

THE NEXT FEW DAYS ARE A BLUR. I GET UP AND GO TO SCHOOL and try to pay attention. Jonah helps me with my homework everyday now, and not just on Tuesdays and Thursdays when the school forces him to. Without him, I'd definitely be falling behind on my grades again, but he keeps me focused.

I feel like I'm walking on eggshells at home. I keep waiting for Mom to say, "It's done. I sold the store." So far, she hasn't said much of anything to me that doesn't involve asking what I want for dinner. She sleeps in late, goes to the store late, and comes home at exactly closing time. I wish I could say I haven't given up, but there's nothing more for me to do. Even with our fundraising sales and all the online marketing in the world, I can't come up with the twenty-three thousand dollars Mom needs to pay off her payday loan.

It's been three days, and that sinking feeling hasn't left my chest. I feel like I'm constantly on the verge of tears, but I hold them back. Jonah and April are being stellar friends and doing everything they can to take my mind off it. I smile and joke with them at lunch and pretend like their efforts are working, but deep down inside, I'm dying.

I can't stand the idea of a life without The Magpie. Even now that I'll definitely graduate with at least B's and maybe even some A's, and with the scholarships Mrs. Reese has gotten for me, my future still feels up in the air. I don't know what to do with myself if I'm not running a business. Jonah assures me I'll figure it out with time, but I'm not so sure.

Mom seems more lost than ever, floating through the house at night like a ghost waiting to sign away their soul. I don't know when the contract signing will happen and our store won't be ours anymore, but I'm sure it'll be soon.

On Thursday, Jonah and I do my homework and then I finish the last of the stack of extra credit papers. It feels like I've climbed Mount Everest when I finally get to drop the completed stack on the table. Nothing can ruin the pride I have over this accomplishment, not even the librarian's annoyed glare at me for making a loud noise.

"You seem a little happier," Jonah says as we move over to the row of computers.

I shrug, not wanting to give a real answer. If I say yes, I'm happier, he'll be able to tell it's a lie. Right now I'm just surviving.

I turn to Jonah and wheel my computer chair right up next to his so that I can rest my cheek on his shoulder. "You make me happy," I say quietly. "Even when life is being stupid, you're still the greatest part of it."

He kisses the top of my head. "You make me more than happy, Nat. I'm still waking up from stress dreams every night where our two months of tutoring are over and you quit hanging out with me."

I snort. "Not happening. I'm taking you with me to college so you can help me study for all of those assignments as well."

"I'd be happy to do that," he says, sliding his hand over to my thigh.

I sit up and decide to check my grades online before logging into ChemXLabs. As I log into the school's website, the top right corner flashes, telling me I have a new email. Our school accounts have email addresses that no one uses except for teachers, who send us assignments and stuff.

I click on it and freeze.

The new email has my dad's name as the sender. The subject line reads: Catching up

I look over at Jonah, but he's checking his own account on the next computer over. My mouth can't seem to form words, so I bat at his arm with my hand until he looks over, one eyebrow raised.

I point to the screen.

He looks confused at first and then says, "Is that your dad?"

"Ex stepdad," I whisper.

He nods once and then puts an arm around me. "What do you want to do?"

"I guess I want to read it," I say, but I move the mouse over to the email and can't bring myself to click it. "Do you think he's being nice?"

"Of course he is, if what Mrs. Reese said is true." Jonah's eyes meet mine. "Do you want me to read it for you?"

I'm about to say yes and jump out of this chair, but I know I need to read it myself. If Mom actually told him to stay out of my life, then I can't be mad at him for obeying her wishes. And I do miss him, after these years. He's the only dad I've ever known.

I click the email.

Hi Natalie,

I hope you can get this email soon. I don't know how often students check these things, but I knew it would be a way to contact you since I don't know your real email address. It's me, Ed, and I wanted to reach out after all this time and make sure you're doing okay.

I miss you a lot, and even though you aren't related to me by blood, please know I still think of you as my daughter. I would be overjoyed if you choose to reply back, or maybe give me a call. Of course, if you don't wish to communicate with me, I will respect that.

You're eighteen now, and almost graduating. I can't believe you've grown up so fast. I still remember when you'd build forts in the living room out of blankets and pretend you were in a spaceship.

I'll be honest, Natalie. Stacy told me she spoke with you and she told you that we'd recently married. I don't know how your mom is doing since she cut off all contact with me, but I hope she is doing well. I want you to know that I'd still very much like to be there for you, in any way you need. Since you are starting college soon, please know I've set aside money for your education since you were a toddler. I'd love to send it your way.

Hope you're doing well. Congratulations on your upcoming graduation, kiddo! I'm so proud of you.

Please call me anytime!
-Ed

JONAH'S HAND SLIDES SLOWLY ACROSS MY BACK. "ARE YOU OKAY?" he whispers after a moment. I nod, struggling against that lump in my throat that makes me want to cry. My stepdad was always a great guy. I don't know what happened between him and my mom, but I don't understand why they had to separate and why he had to leave. Reading his letter makes me wish he'd never left at all.

I stare at that one line in his email, the one about the college money. My tuition at the local state college will be totally paid for if I keep my grades up, thanks to Mrs. Reese's help. Surely, he knows this, since he's married to her now. Why would he even bring it up? He could just keep the money himself and I would have never known.

Jonah and I attempt to do some chemistry work, but as soon as our required tutoring session is over, we both pop out of our chairs, ready to get out of this place. Jonah holds my hand as we walk out of the school and toward his car. He doesn't say anything, doesn't make me talk about what just happened with that email. I am so grateful that he knows when to talk and when to just let me think.

After he's dropped me off at home, I step onto the porch and my feet suddenly feel like they're filled with rocks. I can't step inside. Can't walk up to my room and do something stupid like laundry.

I have to this, and I have to do it now, while Mom is at the store.

I dial the number I still have memorized from when I was a little kid.

"Hello?" he says in this curious way, because my phone number is no doubt unfamiliar to him.

"Dad?" I say, my voice higher than I expect. "It's me. And… well…I need your help."

30

One Month Later

Ed Reese takes one bite of the double chocolate deluxe cupcake and his eyes go wide. "This thing's going to give me diabetes," he says, immediately taking another bite.

"It's not that bad," I say, taking a bite of my own. We're at Gigi's Cupcakes after having our third dinner together since I first called him. This last week has been surreal. Mom and I had a confrontation that was hard, and revealing, and made me sick to my stomach. I eventually forgave her for lying to Ed about me not wanting to see him.

From what I remember of their breakup, he was here one day and then gone the next. They signed the divorce papers separately at the courthouse only two months later, and we never talked again. After my first phone call with my dad last week, I'd asked Mom about it.

She tried to play it off as not a big deal, but it was. To me it was. I told her you can't just keep a girl away from her stepdad when he's done nothing wrong. She cried, and I cried, and eventually we hugged it out.

Luckily, it's only been three years of estrangement, so I don't think we've lost much time together. I'm calling him Dad. It's a little awkward after all these years, but it's what I used to call him before the divorce. It may not be exactly true, but it's better than saying, "Hey there, ex-stepdad!" every time I see him.

"I could go for another one of these," Dad says as he finishes up his cupcake.

I laugh. "I told you they were amazing. I think she sprinkles fairy dust into the icing."

"You said one a week won't kill me, right?" he says, taking a sip of his coffee, which he drinks black just like I do.

I nod. "I mean, it hasn't been medically proven or anything, but I think you'll be fine. I eat them as much as I can afford to."

"Enjoy that teenage metabolism," he says, patting his stomach which isn't even that big. He's maybe ten pounds overweight. "One day you won't be so lucky."

"So Dad," I say, feeling awkward as the name rolls off my tongue. "Why did you and Mom split up?"

It's been a week of getting to know him again. I figure I can ask this burning question now.

He frowns, and little lines appear on his upper lip. "Honey, I don't really know. She told me she didn't love me anymore and kicked me out."

I tear at the edges of my cupcake wrapper. I'd actually figured as much. Mom goes through weird moods and it was like one day she just decided she didn't want to be married anymore.

"Are you okay?" I ask.

"I am now," he says, patting the top of my hand. "It took me two years to get over both losing your mom and you, but when I met Stacy, I felt my heart start to mend back together."

Stacy—or Mrs. Reese as I know her—is actually kind of

okay. Outside of school, she acts like a normal person and doesn't try to lecture me constantly. I can see how she makes my dad happy. She dotes on him and he dotes on her.

The whole thing is weird, but I'm still happy for him.

"You sure your mom is okay?" he asks for the third time today.

I draw in a deep breath and smile. "She will be. The store is saved, so that's really all that matters."

"Good," he says, smiling back at me. "I'm here anytime you need me, kiddo."

His phone buzzes, an incoming call from his office. "Well… except for now," he says with a laugh. "I actually have to go."

I stand up and give him a hug. "See you on Tuesday?" It's his least busy work day and we've agreed to have dinner once a week so we can catch up on things.

"I can't wait."

I wave at him as he leaves Gigi's Cupcakes, but I sit here and sip my coffee for a little while longer. Mom is working at the store, and I'm supposed to relieve her in ten minutes, but for now I just want to sit here and enjoy the feeling of being able to relax.

THAT FIRST NIGHT I CALLED DAD, HE MET ME AT LORENZO'S Pizzeria on the opposite side of town. It was the safest place I could think of where Mom wouldn't accidently show up and catch us talking. We talked for three hours that night. We caught up, we shared stories, we discussed the store.

Turns out my dad had saved over thirty grand for me since I was a baby, and he was happy to let me use the money to pay off Mom's loan under the promise that she won't sell the store to Jack Brown.

Mom was less than thrilled at the idea. But I told her it was my college fund that Dad was going to give me anyway. I spun the idea like it was my own money and I wanted to use it for the store, instead of it being her ex-husband's money that was being used as a shameful bailout.

After a long, arduous argument, Mom finally agreed. She hasn't stopped smiling since we got that awful payday loan off her back. Now we're earning more money than ever thanks to Jonah's efforts, and we don't even need it all to get our bills paid anymore.

And the best part of all?

Jack Brown is gone for good.

Dad had a less than polite talk with him, man to man, about how crappy he was for everything he's done not only to me and Caleb, but to the entire town. Jack's face went beet red and he didn't even argue much by the end of it. Dad tore him a new one, so to speak, and Jack stormed off, promising never to contact us again.

When my coffee is finished, I toss my trash and walk back down the boardwalk toward the store. The smell of the salt water dances in my lungs, and the tune of a bird singing nearby makes me smile. Everything feels better now. The world is more beautiful, and the days are sweeter than ever now that our store is safe, my Dad is back, and Jonah is still the best boyfriend in the world.

Jonah is kneeling next to the chalk board easel outside of The Magpie when I walk up. He's wearing a dark blue Magpie polo shirt my mom gave him.

"What do the ancient pyramids have to do with our book sale?" I ask, squinting at what he's drawn on the board.

"What?" He stands up, taking a step back to admire his work, the chalk pen in his hand. "That's not pyramids. It's a stack of books."

I snort with laugher. "Oh my…Jonah, honey…you are not a

good artist. I might have to ask my mom to rethink her idea of hiring you part time."

He frowns, still looking at the horrible drawing he's made. "It…kind of looks like books?" he says, his lips splitting into a grin. "It looks horrible from this angle."

I take the chalk pen from his hand and pat him on the head. "It's okay, Jonah. You're cute, so I'll try to forgive your terrible drawing skills"

He grabs my hips and pulls me in for a kiss. "Hmm," he says against my lips. "Maybe you should become my tutor this time. Teach me how to draw."

I roll my eyes and wrap my arms around his neck, holding him close. "You are such a nerd."

He grins. "Maybe. But I'm your nerd."

ABOUT THE AUTHOR

Amy Sparling is the bestselling author of books for teens and the teens at heart. She lives on the coast of Texas with her family, her spoiled rotten pets, and a huge pile of books. She graduated with a degree in English and has worked at a bookstore, coffee shop, and a fashion boutique. Her fashion skills aren't the best, but luckily she turned her love of coffee and books into a writing career that means she can work in her pajamas. Her favorite things are coffee, book boyfriends, and Netflix binges.

She's always loved reading books from R. L. Stine's Fear Street series, to The Baby Sitter's Club series by Ann, Martin, and of course, Twilight. She started writing her own books in 2010 and now publishes several books a year. Connect with her on one of the links below.

www.AmySparling.com

facebook.com/authoramysparling

bookbub.com/profile/amy-sparling

goodreads.com/Amy_Sparling